JOHN HOLTEN
THE TRAINS OF EUROPE
Ragnarok III

BROKEN DIMANCHE PRESS

for my mum Candy

Three from the dwelling   at the base of the tree;
One's named Urd   the other's Verdandi
The last is Skuld   & on the wood they scored
Laws they made   & the life allotted
To the children of men   whose fate they sealed.

— *Völuspá, Poetic Edda*

So we beat on, boats against the current,
borne back ceaselessly into the past.

— *F. Scott Fitzgerald*

CONTENTS

Chapter IX 9

The story begins and ends with steam 21

Chapter VIII 25

O to sing of the freedom from the horse 55

Chapter VII 59

*Watch how time and space fold like a sheet
of paper made from pulped trees* 94

Chapter VI.. 99

*We're crying because of all the loss, the losses
ongoing, and the losses to be* 118

Chapter V.. 123

*The ineluctable horror of what happens
next in the tale of the trains* 135

Chapter IV 141

Listen 164

Chapter III... 169

*Even when things are broken and at their worst,
life is conceived and plans are made* 193

Chapter II 197

We tend the world-tree with water and song 230

Chapter I 235

CHAPTER IX

The world above the city is falling into lassitude, the kind borne from summer heat waves. Humid and dense, the hot air weighs down on the rooftop. Luzie's mother moves beneath her to better cradle her head. And she is repeating the words she knows are meant to help her fall asleep: Tomorrow will be better than yesterday. She keeps her eyes closed but still cannot sleep. She feels dizzy from panic when thinking about how high up they are, how her grandmother is not with them, how they are tied to each other, captives. She's got the hunger that makes it hard to sleep properly.

Once it is really dark the older of the two men returns. Maybe he was there all along? Her mother shifts, a line of tension pulling her body beneath taut at the sound of their voices, forcing Luzie to open her eyes and sit up.

The brothers are arguing it appears. Their language is one she has never heard before. Then she looks at her mother who also turns from looking at their two angry captors and mother and daughter hold each other's gaze in the dark. In her mother's face is a message: they are talking to each other silently and Luzie knows it is an important conversation from the lines of concentration on her mother's face.

Ever so slightly, she moves in the dark. There's broken glass near her feet. This makes a scrunching sound. Her mother nods her head as if to indicate behind her, but Luzie knows she's asking about the torch tucked into her trousers at the base of her back and she reaches behind and touches it and yes, it is still there, safe and secret and she nods to her mother. This is when the two men hug each other, having concluded their conversation, and then the tall one looks at them, turns and leaves down the stairs, while his brother stretches out on the old sun chair that sits guard at the roof entrance, crosses his legs, and places his machete carefully on his lap. He closes his eyes.

Her mother waits some time, and when his eyes remain closed she turns, points with her finger behind Luzie to the edge of the roof, draws out a cylinder with her two empty hands and points again. She understands: I'm to take the torch, make it give light, and place it at the edge of the tower. They will trick the man with their magic and they will kill the man so he won't kill them. Then they will be free.

***

The day had started like many before, with hunger. But they had been free. And their trio had still been intact: grandmother, mother, daughter. The world may be without magic and revelry and yet they had this one anomaly – a working torch, a miracle from the world before, when that magic electricity still existed. The world may be wholly profane – one without birthday parties or family holidays, no animated movies or dance routines, no speaking videos or tubby space friends – but they three lay together talking. In their makeshift beds in a trashed room of a large, palatial building, Luzie had asked if they would find her missing father William in the big city. Her mother said they very well might.

And that was when they had heard their captors, down below somewhere in the vast, ruined building.

— Let's leave. Hilda had been the one to make the rapid-fire decision.

— There's a hund, Luzie said to her mother, unsure how bad this information was.

— Luzie! Sybille hissed at her, raising her finger up into the murk in front of her face. You have to be completely silent, you understand?

— What about Maelstrom? The girl said this to herself, but out loud, she needed to hear the words.

As they exited the building from the ground floor, the sound of a berserk cur yapping filled the still air behind them from somewhere inside the building.

— Come on, hurry up. Luzie was whispering to herself. Be quick. Hester quick.

They ran across the wide bridge and continued up the slight incline to where it opened up into a plaza in front of the train station and shopping centre, keeping the canal to their right as it opened out into the Havel lake beyond. This was always going to be risky, with no cover of any kind. But it was the quickest way to leave the town. Cursing, Sybille looked behind her and saw the dog move out of the building.

— Oh fuck, Luzie hold my hand.

— This is no good hund, Luzie whined, this is a dødshund.

There was a tram up ahead, sitting where it had been sitting for years and they rushed into it. The space was full of plastic detritus and mulch leaves and growing grass, the tram's windows half obscured with green growth and layers of dirt, explosions of windblown silicate and insistent ivy. Sybille turned around to force the doors closed.

— Try and find something, anything, and hit the dog!

The doors didn't budge. Outside, the dog was gaining, behind it the figure of a man, long and lithe with a head full of hair, in his hand a long powerful looking blade, running along the tramline meadow.

— Get ready to hit the dog, and as Sybille said this she undid the bundle and grabbed hold of the torch and grabbed Luzie.

— You're going to take this and you're going to hide it. No matter what: you keep this secret.

The girl wriggled as Sybille ran her hand around the seam of her tattered jeans, the bony body of the girl giving her fright as it always did, and stretched them taunt and put the torch down the inline of her back to her bottom, so its form made the girl's jeans fit tightly.

There were two men, as it turned out, and each looked as horrendous as the other: both tall and athletic, bodies each like a highly wrought piece of rope, long hair that ran past their shoulders, beards that one had knotted with some beads, skin dark mahogany from the sun. It was obvious they were brothers: they could have been twins only one looked older, his face more ravaged with the etchings of entropic collapse, and in his hand a long handled blade that suggested he made the decisions. They stood framed by the tram door looking in at them and there was a moment of silence when it was unclear what would happen next, what it was they wanted to gain in their pursuit.

— Warum haben Sie so gelauft? He spoke a rough German.

For years now, you ran when you didn't want anything from people whose path you crossed, and you didn't want them to want anything from you in turn.

He smirked at their silence then turned to the other and spoke words they didn't understand, before picking through Sybille's bundle. They had run dry days before and had nothing of worth. The only item besides the torch Sybille cared about was the book she got as a gift the week the electricity disappeared and which she read and reread as a reminder of that previous world, and her notebook, in which she had been writing since before Luzie was born, which made it six years old.

— I want to take my notebook. Okay? I'm going to go and get my notebook. She raised her eyebrows, tried to let her face be loose and relaxed, unsure if they understood her words or not. She stepped past the older brother, feeling the blood pulse throughout her whole body as she leant and picked up the battered notebook, her longtime talisman, and when she faced him again he had stepped forward so that he was right next to her. She could smell his odour, dank and fetid and rounded out with woodsmoke as he plucked the notebook out of her hand.

He turned it over once, twice, his forehead a crease of lines, his mouth a bow of incomprehension. He opened it and flicked through its pages, looked up at Sybille. Then he tore the book in half, with some difficulty.

— No, fuck. Please. You sonofabitch! Sybille reached to grab the book, to slap it out of his filthy hands and he smacked her clean on the side of the head with such force she fell over.

— Sybille!

— Mama!

As they raised Sybille up he started to tear the notebook apart so that its pages fell around them.

— Komm. Slut bitch, shut up. And he spoke more in his language that sounded to the girl like nothing other than the words of evil itself.

— No please. Crying, Sybille moved out of the arms of her mother and her child and onto her hands and knees, blind almost from her smarting eyes and mucus in her nose, trying to retrieve the pages, marked with her words, dirty glyphs of who she had been and who she dreamed the three of them and William could become in some future that wasn't this future.

Pushing her further away, the man grabbed Luzie and pushed the girl forward, kicking Hilda to move. The three of them stumbled and turned to walk away from the scene, Sybille the slowest, looking back at the mess of the ransacked belongings. Of all the eventualities she had feared she hadn't imagined the loss of her notebook and the book *To Warmann,* the only items she had allowed herself to claim possession over.

The three of them were bound together with old cable wire. Their horse had been found and the younger brother now rode on it ahead of them, while the older brother walked behind them. They were following the railroad which headed into the city, a dozen or so kilometres away. By afternoon they were in the city proper, the tracks now cut into the earth, two wide escarpments fanning out either side and lined above with trees, apartment buildings whose windows were all punctured with cattail stalks growing on windowsills. Up ahead was the treeline of what had been a park. When they crossed a bridge, the buildings of Potsdamer Platz came into view, a cluster of towers that stood unbending and plumb, the tallest one catching the orange light of the setting sun in its upper windows so that it looked like it had been painted, a calling beacon left unanswered.

The sound from the built environment was ethereal and tremulous: for kilometres stretched out roads and streets and built surfaces from which sunk cellars and basements and underground areas and sealed rooms, bunkers, tunnels and pipeways, above which rose buildings, rooms and corridors and stairwells, all empty and sighing in the slow, convective heat of summer and through all these spaces animals and humans moved over broken glass and debris, wind whistling low and strumming vibrations outward so that the place sounded different than the open countryside: here, the sound was of nature slowly reasserting itself in the cracks of artificially compressed matter, the baked minerals of human artifice. A hum with an intermittent discordance: straining, it was possible to hear faint shouting far off, the sound of distress or censor.

They approached the black yawn of a tunnel mouth into which the railroad descended. The long, inert body of an ICE train sat on the tracks, half in the tunnel. It had long ago been burned out and ruined, ivy ran over much of its length. Just as the caravan passed the tunnel's lip, pigeons exploded out of the gloom, breaking the clip clopping of the horse as they flew out of the tunnel.

They continued on in dogged silence. After a while platforms of an underground train station could be made out by the different tone of black and the opening up of the horse's clip-clop into a wider notation. There was an acrid smell of burned plastics and the air was harsh and Sybille spat loudly, tasting also as she did the ferric twang of her own blood. Anhalter Bahnhof. They kept going, the older brother was leading them now based on acoustics only. The dark was total.

When they reached another underground station, this one larger than the last, the older brother hauled himself up onto the platform. Everyone stopped when they heard his movement, their eyes taking longer than they normally did to adjust to the penumbra that was seeping through from somewhere up ahead.

Daylight came down the large stairwell and they moved toward this navy blue light, the chasmic space of the railway station opening above them. The two entranceways to the underground station had been housed in large square porticos made of stout metal columns and glass walls and ceilings. When they came up the stairs and out onto the platz, late summer evening all about them, they saw that the entranceway opposite them had collapsed, as if a giant had thrown something on it from above.

It was not obvious why they decided to kill Hilda here at this moment, after making her walk all that way. Then they made the last two survivors of this family, mother and daughter, trudge up twenty-six floors of stairs to the roof, the apex where the jaded red *DB* sign was still intact on its glass façade.

***

She loosens the cord and frees herself from her mother and stands. It is so dark now she is not afraid. She moves silently over the broken glass and looks out across the city and she stills herself the better to see the tiny pin pricks of light where a few fires and torches burn. They are few and far between and resemble stars in the sky: she stares hard at the few still blinking in the darkness, imagining that they are communicating to her some- how, telling her what she should do or what will happen.

— Where the summerbirds have gone to. She is whispering to herself: Father maybe, waiting for me. Yesterday was better than today.

She then turns around to look where the man sits, their jailor. She can't see him properly but only hears where he breathes, the fabric of his clothes making the slightest of rustling sounds. She walks until she feels open space ahead of her, a slight tremor up ahead where the roof ends and the drop begins. With her hand, she feels the low ledge that marks the roofside, the glass panes from the building façade running alongside it. This she can grip like a handrail and she leans her body over it, and feels the air and the black expanse that yawns below. She turns and looks back to where she can just about make out the figure of the older brother and then she turns and looks back out toward the in- visible city shrouded in night. Every move she makes is watched by her mother who sits like a ragdoll statue faking sleep.

The torch is still between her trousers and her skin, she has grown used to it after all these hours and now she slowly retrieves it and holds it in her hands and thinks of all that has happened since she first saw it do its magic. Her fingers run over it and she turns it in her hands before she finally finds the small button that she applies pressure to, knowing that's how its strange, otherworldly currency is activated. A beam of light cuts the air, filling the space below the device, lighting up her thin legs and the ledge and the ground of the roof that is filled with broken glass and detritus. Its luminescence is like a siren: its muteness startling. She swallows, excitement trembles up from her stomach and her mouth fills with saliva. She swallows again. Then she turns the torch over so that its shaft of light also moves, pointing up to the stars, and she reaches over and places it on the ledge, just by the glass façade, and steps backwards, walking away though not taking her eyes off the incredible sight of the yellow-orange wedge. As she backs up against the wall, near where her mother waits, she hears the brother exclaim and scramble to his feet, muttering in short bursts of astonishment at what he is seeing. He moves quickly, almost fearfully, toward the beam of light, ignoring Sybille and Luzie as he steps past them.

Luzie is happy to see him fall for the trick, his body transformed now into a stark black outline against the light. As she stares, holding her breath, he raises his arm to pick up the torch and as he does so she pushes herself forward and runs headlong to him, her little arms hitting him in his stomach and the shock of her attack takes him completely by surprise so enraptured is he by the mechanism in his hands and his body, top heavy, goes over the edge, a foot hitting Luzie in the side of the head, and falls over and down in an instant, the torch along with him. He lets out a wail, a curse, a scream, and Luzie leans over and looks at the shadow of his body as the torch's tumbling beam cleaves the night as it too tumbles and turns as if the world is submerging into black water, the frontage of the building glowing in close up before the arc swings out into the dark night, tumbling and falling and disappearing, until quiet rises up with the return of blackness.

The story begins and ends with steam.

The three of us first bring water to the world-tree.

We wish to tell of the technologies and destinies of children.

So start with the steam engine, made to pump water out of an extraction mine, then later to power what comes to be called a train. A man named James Watt is the engineer who first understands that there is a need for a sink, for what is lost in the creation of so much heat, otherwise a closed engine system, you see, will explode and break down and drive nothing forward.

To move something you have to let something go, just as to tell a story you must leave something out.

When the sea comes up to meet the sky, this story is truly over. Until then we have steam, the barking of a dog, the saga of horses growing happy and sad.

You see, if you hear us out, you'll understand the fate of the sun, which is to say how you, and everything else, will meet your timely end.

You humans surround yourself with hyperobjects, things whose beginnings or ends you can neither read nor see but only intuit, and only then in nightmares or faceless bureaucracy, all those other gradients of your beloved progress, laws and innovations.

Beyond the tale's Berlin origin lies a world-machine to be mapped out and comprehended, and it starts with a need to overcome a dependence on horses. It is the age of Napoleon – and yes of course we need to look at the actions of men in times of war, you shouldn't be surprised. There is a man who dies from cholera, the plague that takes no time at all, and he is buried a pauper with all his earthly possessions including his words. His name is Carnot. After the cataclasm of Waterloo, Carnot sets about understanding the workings of steam, this power source that gave the advantage to the British. His only book, which nobody read when he was alive, is one origin for this telling of beginnings and endings, its title a swirl itself of poetic possibility: Reflections on The Motive Powers of Fire.

Within its unread pages lies planted the seed for your understanding of why things fall apart, why one thing happens after another, why there is a past, a present and a future and why you cannot move from the latter to the former. Your lives, like so many of your stories, are linear. But we're here to tell you that they don't have to be. Carnot's big discovery is the science of thermodynamics, that heat flows from hot things to cold things and never from cold things to hot things and, crucially, that some-thing is always lost in the creation of energy. What is lost like the dreamed next step in the instant after awakening, or the memory of birth.

Thanks to Carnot we begin to understand thermo-dynamics, we understand that the sun also will grow cold and, like all stars, it too will die.

And so we go ever on.

CHAPTER VIII

The passing is their chosen route to the river for it gives the best protection from prying eyes. It runs over a gentle hill, a laneway of knee-length grass she has been flattening, and is protected on both sides with thick green coppiced chestnuts. Usually, Sybille walks through it twice a day: once in the morning for ablutions and then again in the evening to rinse their jaded cutlery. This evening wind sways the verdure and beyond its susurrus is a rhythmic clanging from the settlement that lies beyond on the south bank of the river, two families from the west whose lives have been taken over by religion. They have traded a little with them but each group has made it clear they prefer to be left alone.

She steps lightly and with speed and when she reaches the riverbank she spends time scanning the banks on either side and in either direction. Eyes, she feels a pair of eyes on her and she thinks: William, if ever you were going to return to us please make it sometime soon. She says aloud alone to no one:

— Please come back.

She puts the basin down by the water on the wide bend of the meander and the sedge and slurp of mud secures it from the current. Squatting down, with exaggerated care she begins to wash the dishes and her mind goes blank and calm descends, the clanging ceases and the only noise is the talk of birds and a quiet conversation between the wind and water. The three plates and sets of knives and forks are soon clean. She reaches and pulls up a handful of grass and loosely twists the leaves into a primitive plait which she then flings out over the slate green water and they fan out, disperse. She takes her time watching them turn slowly on the water surface and sink. This ritual of dishwashing is pointless really but she needs it: increasingly she is finding it hard to show calm, especially at the adaptability of Luzie and how this punishing world with their mendicant routines is now wholly normal for the girl: the grey veil of danger that clings to empty space agitating with possibility, the always imminent danger of attack or sickness or some other reversal of fortune. There are so many unnameable events that are possible in all childhoods, she tells herself. Are Luzie's any different really? Could she compare? This is Luzie's known world, she knows no other and as her mother it is her duty to deal with that fact. It is the presence of her own mother that saves her, Sybille knows that.

The feeling of someone watching her returns and she looks up and across the slowly turning arc of the river to the bank opposite. Nothing stirs. Above the treeline a thin wisp of smoke but otherwise nothing. The sky is growing dark and dusk sits all about in the quiet air. She moves quickly up through the passing and keeps her eyes fixed straight ahead half expecting to see a figure emerge from bush and tree. The trees sway on the top of the hill, the wind picking up as coolness sets in. When she passes over the crest she can see their compound, the white of the gable and brown of the two outhouses and something to its aspect gives her fright, something immediately feels ajar and that the world is somehow not right. She doesn't realise that she is running until she nearly topples over at the rate of descent down into the courtyard.

— Luzie! Mother!

The small figure of her daughter appears out of the back door of the house. The girl stands blinking with a frown on her face, alarm is so normal for her.

— Where's grandmother? Luzie! Where is she? Has anybody been here?

She throws the basin down roughly so that it hits the ground by the door, barely holding its contents, and she runs into the gloom of the house, shouting as she does so.

— Mother?

It is almost dark in the rooms and she passes through the dusty spaces quickly but knows already what she intuited up in the passing: something has come through their little outpost and raised it up in the time she had been to the river – what, twenty minutes if even? – and when placed back down on the earth something is no longer sitting right. The house is too silent. Not now, not mother – these words repeating in her mind– not without William back.

She moves through the house, ignoring the trailing presence of her daughter and she catches herself and is surprised but not really surprised – a forgotten resignation – that she is in danger of hyperventilating.

— Luzie! What's happened?

The girl stands stunned a bit of ways from the back door.

— Nothing. I don't know. Nothing happened. Her voice is starting to rise, a mix of indignation and fear. I was in the yard and granny was in here. Then she wasn't.

— What do you mean "then she wasn't"? she walks past Luzie and into the middle of the courtyard, not waiting for an answer.

— Mother! Mother! She draws the last call out and is shocked and scared by how frightened she sounds, fright mixed with a fatigue fraught with resignation and debilitating loss. There is no response and the night is upon them and only some last bird is audible. The overgrown land, the course of the river, the expanse of Europe: all are being overcome with nighttime as the sun recedes west.

— Maybe she went over to the field? To pick berries? But there aren't berries yet, it's too early... She is speaking rapidly, quietly, to herself and stops and frowns into the dark of the treeline and thinks about the possibilities. They have not had any visitors in the time they've been at the farmstead. Why would mother go to the field or anywhere beyond the calling range of Luzie? Those eyes she felt on her by the river, was that just coincidence?

— Fuck.

Back inside the house, she gets the lamp and matches, waterproofed with candle wax just the night before and some of the last they have. Everything, they have always to remind themselves, is finite including the possibility of light in the dark.

— Come on, let's see if she walked down the lane.

She takes her daughter's hand and she strides in big determined steps, suddenly impatient and forcing the girl to half run and the speed increases both their anxieties. They pass through the gateway between the two outhouses and there is still light enough to see easily although everything is rapidly becoming indistinct and enveloped in darkness. A little further and she stops suddenly, pulling on Luzie's arm hard, frozen with the terror one has when another animal is present that has no right to be present, the terror of the arachnophobe on seeing a spider in a bathtub. But this is no spider in front of them, it is a huge horse over fifteen hands tall. Clearly well trained, it stands placid on the edge of the laneway under the foliage of the hedgerow and it is this animal and nothing else she realises now which made her feel something was not right when she returned through the passing – she must have kenned the animal but only out of the corner of her eye, protected as it is through the wall of trees and bush.

Calmly, the horse blusters through its nostrils and lifts up its left hoof before placing it back down only in turn to raise its right hoof as if debating with herself to bolt but remaining out of servile curiosity. Then the horse nickers and nods their long face once, twice. Sybille is struck with terror and her terror is picked up by the child and she feels her skin grow cold from the onset of adrenaline. Luzie stands obediently beside her, looking from her mother to the horse, aware that danger lies everywhere and now is not the time to speak, nor to make a single movement, to be anything other than her mother's silent shadow. They have been in such situations before.

— Come on, this way, she whispers and turns around and moves as lightly as she can back into the compound, surveying the three buildings as she does so, passing in front of the main outhouse and out through the way behind the farmhouse into the field. The field is the name they give to the undulating expanse of former farmland that stretches out west and that follows the course of the river to the south. They talked before about what to do in case of attack or any form of unwelcome or unannounced visitation and the plan changes depending on which direction any visitation would come, and the main procedure they agreed upon is as simple as it is crude – they will run in the opposite direction of the intrusion. The field offers some cover with its long grasses and sporadic copses, as well as vantage points to look back upon the compound itself and survey the movements and numbers of any pursuers. But why would she leave Luzie and herself behind? And why would the horserider not have already made themselves known? She stops after a few paces into the long grass of the field and hunkers down, putting down the lamp and taking a hold of the child.

— Luzie, what happened? What did you hear when I was at the river?

— Nothing. I, I, I was in the courtyard. And ...

— And you didn't hear or see anything?

— No.

— And grandmother didn't call out or appear at any time?

— No. You left and I went out to the courtyard. That's it.

The girl is desperate but knows not to cry.

— Okay. But we have to find granny now.

She shakes her head in the dark. Swallows uncomfortably. She's been addressing herself more than the child. Light the lamp, she tells herself. Because it is almost full night and she still hasn't the hang of the thing to do it in the impenetrable darkness – like so much else – and she pauses a moment until she is sure it has caught and then rises and searches out the child's hand and they walk out into the sea of darkness.

— We're going to go as far as we can and see if –

She cuts herself short and hunkers back down, blows out the lamp and, still crouching down, grabs Luzie and holds her breath and her daughter does the same, their heads just reaching out of the long grass and the blackness of night weighing all around them. There is no sound she can place that doesn't belong to the landscape of gloaming and the sighing wind that is increasingly picking up.

— This way, she whispers and they scurry, still crouching, and with difficulty move through the thick wildflowers and grasses, to the first copse that the untilled land offers. She is desperate beyond sensible thought and the adrenaline streaming through her body makes it hard for her to remain calm, to even be still or hear clearly, blood merging and thumping behind her ears. Nothing stirs in the night and the silence is more than she can bear. They are more at risk than ever. She holds her breath once more and places both hands on her daughter's shoulders in an effort to bring stillness to her overly alert body. Straining her eyes to see anything at all in the disappeared fields, all she can make out is hedgerow, the clump of coppice merging into the darkness that is now all around them. Sound the dominant sense the darker it gets.

— Mum?

— Shhh!

She turns and looks back at where the compound is, no more than half a kilometre away but already lost. Nothing moves: no body nor any point of lambency. She thinks she sees a pinprick of luminescence but it is gone before she even tells herself it is a firefly. The cumulus cloudbanks from earlier are now slowly breaking apart and she wonders how long it will take for the crescent moon to appear.

— Let's walk as quietly as we can further up the field, okay? We're going to find granny, don't worry. We just have to be extra quiet. Extra careful.

A last skylark chitters and grows silent as mother and daughter stand and then start slowly to put one foot in front of another, their steps high and effortful and at the same time pressing as little weight on the earth as possible, as though trying to suck in any sound that they might emit. Studying the sky, Sybille sees that to the north the clouds have parted and in that lighter, ink-coloured section of sky lie two blinking coordinates of activity, infinitely distant and remote: Venus chasing the crescent moon and Aldebaran, the orange star. The latter she has often looked for in the blackness, in the constellation of her star sign, the night of her birth, 31 years previous, giving her this affinity to the eye of the bull. The clouds will keep parting, she tells herself. That will give more light and her eyes will grow in strength from the lightening.

Moving is hard in the dark – too quick risks being discerned against the frozen formlessness of night, too slow risks being caught. But on they go, slowly, Sybille's left arm half raised involuntarily, the other clasping the hand of her trembling daughter.

Until a noise pierces the silence and they stop.

It was like a call but it wasn't clear and it wasn't her mother.

There it is again, the same indistinct calling. And then Sybille sees there's another person in the field, over toward the compound. It isn't grandmother.

They are still peering into the nothingness when a low beam of light emanates from a circle coined as if by magic and then fans out in a wondrous cylinder of light and sweeps with a jerk once, twice, as if searching for a bearing in the cornerless dark.

An electrical torch.

As soon as it is there, it is blinking out, its disappearance plunging everything back to a black, which feels a shade darker than before.

The last time Sybille saw such light was seven years before.

— Mummy, she spoke loudly, confused and distracted. What was that?

— That's a torch, an electrical one. And I can't believe it. But we've got to hide Luzie, we've got to go.

There is a swale further north that has some growth and they can reach it before whoever is in ownership of the torch can close the distance between them.

— Come on, she says, and now they're moving quickly and find the bushes and get down onto the ground, their legs tucked under them, the girl whimpering from the presence of nettles but forces herself to be quiet.

Then the light returns, its bright coin source closer than before, to the east, to their right, before disappearing again. The same indistinct call. They are fast, whoever they are. And alone. Or at least that much Sybille hopes.

When the light coins again, it is shining in the opposite direction – toward the river to the south – and the silhouette of its bearer is there to see: he's tall and slightly bent, like a transom under too much weight. The light shaft jerks east to west then blinks off. In the moments that follow, there is first silence across the land, until he calls out, again with the same indistinct entreaty.

The light blinks on again, further west now and closer to them, along the slope of the land.

Time passes in heartbeats rushed with adrenaline. The light comes on and off, exposing tracts of land as it does so. He is headed west, if erratically; he would have to backtrack to find them. But it was not impossible. When the land is dark once more she almost bundles Luzie and makes a run for it to the compound. But what then? Could she ride that horse with Luzie? Could they mount it and turn it quick enough and leave without making sure her mother is not there?

Flat panic as she strains her ears and eyes across the field.

And then – light, as she has forgotten it could manifest. It passes across the space and exposes them where they crouch, stunning them to immobility when really they should be running. She thinks of the rabbit they snared the day before ruefully: old sayings of the electric world always have a mocking tone to them and now more than ever.

— Halt, bleiben, he says, in a German accented with French.

She is shaking and clutching her daughter so tightly that the girl starts to protest. The end shouldn't be drawn out like this, it is supposed to be quicker: in her nightmares it has always been as fast and unexpected as a slap from a stranger.

The light flips off and he speaks once more:

— No danger, he says in English.

— Where's my mother?

— She's fine, she's back at the house.

— Then why isn't she here? What do you want from us? We have no food, any we do have you can take.

— I don't want food. He is half shouting now, in his heavily accented English. I'm here because William sent me.

Sybille coughs from the unexpected words.

— William? Where is he?

The adrenaline in her has changed course; it is flooding back up toward her chest and face. She feels her body temperature change. And then the light returns and plays up toward the sky. It shines in the man's face, giving Luzie a start: he looks demonic in the electric light surrounded by so many years of darkness. The light itself seems supernatural, casting his features in shadows that draw him like a ghoul. Sybille stands and Luzie follows her example.

The three of them stand facing one another out in the field.

— My name is Koby.

— I don't care what your name is. What do you want from us? What have you done to my mother?

— She's back at the house. Ecoutez, William is fine too. He sent me here –

— Where is he? Is he dead? She shouts this, stepping a pace toward him as if she will hit the man if he doesn't tell her what she wants to know.

— He's ok. He told me to tell you that he's not going to become your Warmann, or disappear forever. He said you would understand. He isn't dead, Sybille. Let's just go back to the house and I can tell you everything calmly.

Warmann. Her biggest fear has been that he was not coming back. Over and over, she kept asking for him not, dear lord, to become Warmann. Simply not knowing was worse than if he were dead.

— Oh my god, is all she says. Then she steps forward. She places her hands on Luzie's shoulders, steers the girl ahead of her, caution abandoned.

— Yes, that's what he told me to tell you. He said you wouldn't trust me and that should be enough to placate you.

The man speaks in long, undulating sentences that seem pushed into English straight from the French and she is having trouble following him or indeed listening to him as her mind processes that here is an emissary from William and she shakes as the adrenaline fully switches course from fear to relief.

— He even made me write down the name! he adds, laughing mirthlessly. Then he turns off the torch and they are plunged back into darkness.

— But where is he exactly? Is he ok? Why didn't he come himself?

— He's fine. Come, let's go back to the house.

— And how do you have electric light?

— I'll tell you all.

— You go first. We follow.

The man pauses, then moves ahead with an exaggerated shrug of his shoulders as if it was all the same to him. Sybille and Luzie follow a couple of paces behind. The clouds are being dispersed by the wind now, exposing more sky which contains some light from the crescent moon and emerging Milky Way, so that their surroundings are visible again: the land, the compound and beyond it the course of the hillock, the slumbering river. The expanse of the field seems larger and, in the washed-out vision of Sybille's night-adjusted eyes, it appears just then to be endless. She admonishes herself that he caught them so easily, she should have just kept running.

By the time they reach the compound light is emanating from the back room and it irks her that this stranger is so adept already at navigating what had been their home and sanctuary. She thinks about the horse, and fleeing, but knows that the promise of news of William, and her missing mother, means she'll do no such thing. Slowly, they enter the room staring at the torch that stands upright in the centre of the table, transfixed by its existence and its beam, as if it is a thing to touch or fear or listen to.

— Okay, let's all rest calm. In fact, your mother ran away but I am sure she will come back and –

— You fucker! What do you mean, you said she was here.

Sybille lunges then, grabs the torch and shines it at him, pushing the child away into the far side of the room.

— What do you want? she asks him.

— Calm yourself.

— Run upstairs, Luzie. You know what to do.

The child whimpers and stumbles as she walks backwards toward the stairs. The light exposes the man in stark contrasts and his long arms fan out either side of him as if the light is pinning him to the wall.

— Listen, Sybille. Trust me, I mean you no harm, just listen to me. I met William around two months ago and we became friends –

— Friends? Nobody just becomes friends. Not anymore.

— I come from a community with electricity.

— How is that possible?

— Yes it is true, and so things are different for us. I do not lie, Sybille. We are friends. We should be friends too.

— Where is William?

— He told me all about you, your mother and Luzie and together we set out about a week ago to you –

— Then where the fuck is he now?

— Berlin. Perhaps. Probably.

— Berlin? She is growing hysterical because after so long here is a lifeline to William's existence – this stranger knows her name, he knows enough to make it likely he is a friend of William. But too many things still don't add up: the horse, the silent disappearance of her mother, his lying and fooling them into the house, into what feels now like little more than an all too obvious trap. Taking a step back, she grabs a knife from the side-board by the kitchen door, the very same with which she skinned the rabbit the day before.

— Don't you take one step, you son of a bitch. I'll stab you. I'll kill you stone dead. Now you better explain quickly how he ended up with you.

— Please, calm. Look, it's hard for me to fully explain quickly. We were riding for a few days when he decided to go to Berlin because that's where his family was –

— Bullshit! We're his family! He was going to Berlin to begin with. I don't understand how he met you, what he was doing so far west.

She shakes the torch in her hand indicating the phenomenon of electric light, the many truncated rumours of so many dark byways.

— When he reached our community he had already changed his plan. Something to do with his brother–

— Brother? That's where he was going. His brother was in Berlin.

She is crying with frustration and confusion.

— He had been with us for a month or so, regaining strength. Winter had almost killed him and when he turned up he was in bad form. Very bad. We became friends. He told me about you, his family, and how he had left you here to find out about the communities with electricity. He wanted to return to this compound and I decided to come with him as it is safer when you are two.

— So where the fuck is he! She is screaming but still registers that Luzie is moving above her on the first floor. She can't forget the child.

— Some days ago I awoke, he was gone. We had argued about what to do. My guess is he went to Berlin. I thought maybe he might come here. It was hard for me to find, mais voilà, I found it.

None of this is making any sense and between loud sobs she tells him as much.

— He had it marked on the map where you were on the river. I knew I could get here in some days if I found the river. When I arrived, I scared your mother in the lane and she ran into the trees before I could reassure her. I went after her but she hid too well. Then I heard your calls. I mean you no harm, Sybille. I know it is a lot to hear and to believe. But it is true. All of it.

At that moment comes the noise of Luzie opening the window upstairs, then the girl shouting down to her mother.

— Mormor is outside, mama! She's here!

Sybille stares into the face of Koby, who now stands before her with what she tells herself is a forced expression that implores her to believe he means her no harm. Calculation and intuition stream between their gazes and she stops crying, her breathing coming to a regular rhythm so that her thoughts can come to her in order.

— Why would I want to hurt you and come all this way when I have that? He gestures to the torch.

— That's exactly what I am asking myself.

He sighs with frustration.

— The world as we knew it may have ended with the darkening but all is not lost. Electricity: it is possible once more. You hold it in your hand, for god's sake.

— Are you religious?

— No, he says and laughs, confused.

— Mama! Are you out there? Sybille shouts so suddenly that Koby jumps and she raises the knife at a higher angle in response to him moving at all.

— Mama? She continues, speaking now in Norwegian, in what she hopes is a neutral tone.

— He says he knows William and means us no harm but I don't trust him.

— If he's standing, get him to sit at the table. Then I'll come in.

— Sit down there, she says indicating with the knife, all the while holding his gaze with her own. She keeps it on him as he moves slowly, pulling the chair nearest to him and then sitting, his hands on the table's laminate surface.

— Okay he's sitting, come in.

The door opens and its opening feels like a correction to the brash closing of it by the man, who looks now from Sybille to the figure entering the room. Hilda is holding the hand axe they use for wood and its compact weight gives a gravity to the man's position. Sybille thinks she can see him trying to look more relaxed by tilting his head to the side, nodding to himself ever so slightly and then speaking:

— Hi there.

— So, what do you want?

Her mother is poised, almost appearing unfazed. Sybille has come to depend on this naturalness. Hilda's small stature is filled out by the straightness of her back and the set expression of her face, her eyebrowless eyes of crystal grey, startling below the long white of her single-plaited hair. Sybille feels like her mother is of another time in this time that is itself quite other.

Daughter and mother don't look at each other for they have no need: they have done similar interrogations before. Children, lost and orphaned, men, women, young and old – caught stealing their possessions in the moments before dawn at a bivouac, or fellow travellers on the roads who violated their space. It was in the north that they developed the method of departing before their intruders knew they had left. While it was hard to reward the greed of the interloper, the thief, the rapist, it worked: the inverse of pre-darkening logic means that they can escape the immediate moment to ensure survival in the long term.

The trouble always is how to get a head start.

— I mean you no harm, says the man. I'm sorry I scared you in the lane.

— You did not scare me, I simply do not know you. I gave up talking to men I don't know long ago.

— That's fair.

— Now tell us how you got that torch, where is it from? It's true then, what we heard about? The east has electricity?

— Mama, he says he knows William!

Now both women look at each other.

— He knew our names, adds Sybille.

— Perhaps he can tell us then how he knows our names.

— Yes, yes, no problem, I can tell. He has made the

43

mistake of interrupting the grandmother, with his magician's assurance, tinged with the slippery sounding Frenchness of his English.

— I can tell everything, everything.

— Maybe he should begin at the beginning? What do you think, Sybille?

The two women look at each other and the younger of them hesitates, trying to figure out any strategy that her mother might be deploying. She nods her head silently.

— What's your name again? Hilda takes out the chair opposite the man and draws it to the far corner of the room and sits on it.

— Koby.

— Okay then Koby, maybe you should tell us everything you can. Right from where you were before the darkening up to when you rode in here on your horse.

The man sniffs. Blinks once, twice, as if he is suddenly unsure of himself. Then he looks from mother to daughter who is still standing in the very same spot since when he closed the door on her five minutes before.

— Go on, speak! Sybille shouts, bringing everyone back to a state of heightened alertness.

— What do you want me to tell? Where –

— Start at the beginning. Where you were born.

— D'accord, he says, pinching his nose and sniffing again, I was born in Paris, my parents were from Africa. Cameroon and Congo. And he asks with a flourish: whatever the hell happened to Africa in all this? Maybe it's doing better than ever before? Anyway, I went to a shit school and had shit friends but I was smart enough

44

to realise that if I was ever going to live a life worth living I would have to work twice as hard because the banlieues were whirlpools you couldn't escape from. All the clichés, he says, suddenly sounding irate. So I ended up studying in the L'X, the École Polytechnique. Yes. I am an engineer, like William. Or at least I had been, he adds, waving his arm to indicate everything that intervened between him and his profession. My life had been pretty much a good life. Education, the possibility of a good job. Then by the time of l'obscurité, when the darkening came, I had a girlfriend, you know, real good career prospects. I had even reconciled myself to France and my parents, my place in a racist world and – he lets a pause grow before continuing brightly – we were some of the first to know. He turns to face each woman in turn. At L'X, at the Polytechnique, in those first hours, days.

— The first to know what?

— The fact that it wasn't just going to be a blackout that would be fixed with some repairs or a rebooting of the system.

His voice speeds up, the sentences tumbling out as he speaks of the first nights camping out at his school and worrying about his girlfriend, his parents, his friends, but not wanting to leave the vicinity of the laboratories where tests and measurements, a rudimentary search for answers, were being carried out.

— Luzie! Bring down a candle! Sybille breaks the man's monologue. She hates the image of these experts in the dark. The advent of loss. At the same time, she wants to believe so much that the world still has something to give in the form of this man telling the truth. That's why she interrupted him and now she wants her daughter by her side.

The child comes down the stairs and enters quietly with two candles in her hands, staring with fright at the man at the table, her eyes wide yet squinting in the presence of the miracle of electric light. Sybille passes her the matches as the man continues.

— When I realised that there was going to be no immediate solution, I decided to try and find Diana, my girlfriend, she lived in Belleville in the north of the city. My idea had been we could go to the south where her parents lived... He trails off into silence before picking up again: I wasn't prepared for the chaos waiting beyond the Polytechnique, you know. What I'd see. Nobody within had talked much about the general public's reaction, everyone's mind was focused on the gossip and rumour of the laboratories, the technicians and the communications from the government being dispatched by foot. Some people got a kick out of those first days, he scoffs and shakes his head as if recalling a fond memory. People were excited like children. My friend Philippe had volunteered to run a message to the Elysee Palace. Pfff. Never saw him again. He clears his throat before adding: This delay probably saved my life, but it meant I lost everyone.

— What delay? Hilda asks.

— The delay of two or three days when I thought the catastrophe would be solved by my colleagues and teachers! He laughs with embarrassment tinged with ruefulness. Everyone in the room falls silent. The child has put a candle beside her grandmother on the counter by the sink.

— Go on, says Sybille. What happened when you left?

He shakes his head and looks down at the table.

— Sprichst du Deutsch? Do you speak German? Bla bla. Or whatever it is that's spoken around here? I bet you don't. But who cares because what do any of us speak anymore? There's so little that tied us together, those of us with a memory. When the lights went out we all lost it. There are two types of people since: those who stay put and those like you and me who move. Those that stay put die quicker and influenza was already waiting its turn when I started to move.

— People were already getting sick within a week?

— Not with influenza but with everything else. I mean, what do you want to know? How I scurried like a rat once it was dark, crossing the city street by street, already knowing that even if I wasn't shot I still would never see my girlfriend, my family, my friends again? Each arrondissement had a different curfew, different set of rules. The first talk of the English crossing the channel because of the collapse of the power plant Hinkley Point and its radiation. Language became such a currency. Who would have thought?

— I don't really follow what you're talking about, Hilda speaks by way of answer.

— You are three women so you suffer the threat of rape, physical weakness, in relation to others. Yes? I'm a black man so I suffer being worth less and more easily … pffft! He makes a sudden flick of his left hand, as if throwing something over his shoulder. The old world was a game but it was a polite game. There was so many of us, so many people, it was only normal some would cheat and many would be losers. Now that there are so few of us remaining … well, the politeness has gone. In Paris, in L'isle de France surrounding it, people retreated into ever smaller groups they could identify with. Almost immediately.

The two women frown and look at each other. The little girl crinkles up her nose, a sign she fails to understand the words of adults.

— Are you talking about how you survived? asks Sybille.

— Did you pretend to be English, is that it?

— No, no, that's not it at all. I was already heading south when the English arrived and the chaos of their departure from their islands is something I managed to escape. But I heard about it. What were they to do? Stay and be radiated? They were scared. So they came to France any way they could. There were battles, fights. Then the influenza came. Hunger. His eyes are gleaming now from the candle and he no longer raises his head to look at them. So much death.

— Tell us about electricity. Where are you coming from? How many of you are there?

— Not many.

— And how did you manage it?

— Small batteries are possible, small circuits. They're working on making them bigger.

He grows reticent, despondent as both women start to grow impatient.

— Where did you meet William?

— Near Aachen, a series of villages that have electricity, the first I believe you come across from the east. William turned up one day. He knew enough about engineering that he was tolerated. We became friends. He was in a bad way. Close to dying, I guess.

— I find it hard to believe you: why would you just become friends, just like that? And he's dying? It doesn't make sense.

The man lets out a long sigh.

— That's how it was. Believe me or don't believe me. Je m'en fiche.

— But I just don't understand: you said he left for Berlin?

— We had gone too far north from here and he had heard how Berlin had got electricity and self organised. He talked about going to look for his brother –

— But he left us to go to Berlin. Why would he then end up in the west? Why are you lying to us?

Her daughter goes to put her hands around Sybille's waist. Because Sybille is crying now.

— You understand that this doesn't give us much to go on, says Hilda. We don't know you and therefore we cannot trust anything you say.

— I understand.

— But the fact that you come with electricity in your hand and know William means we cannot just send you away. I suggest we all go to sleep and in the morning, with daybreak, we talk about what to do next. You will sleep upstairs. There are a number of beds, take your pick. We will stay down here, the three of us. If you need to go to the toilet, do it now, go outside.

— D'accord, he says after a moment. All I will say is: I don't know why exactly he left like he did. We argued about where to go next, then went to sleep. When I woke up he was gone. I wanted to find you. To give you the possibility of finding him.

Nobody speaks for a few moments. Koby seems lost in his own thoughts, an impression Sybille puts down to calculation. Then he nods and goes out the door, the tense threat of before dissipated and gone. Luzie moves into the kitchen and starts to decant water. Mother and daughter stand and stare at each other wordlessly and Sybille sighs because she knows that this is just the prelude to their set course of action: they will leave this man here and they will leave this compound, like birds leaving their nest. The scent and disturbance will never be eradicated, eggs unhatched or squawking fledglings – the price paid for what has been altered. Who knew that trust made up so much of what it means to be human?

When he comes back in, Hilda speaks.

— One last thing, what did William have with him when he left? Do you think he had what it takes to reach Berlin?

— Yes he had what it takes. Also a horse.

Later when they hear him take the bed nearest the stairs and take off his boots and lie down and his breath steadies until snoring emanates from his bed they exchange their brief conclusions, align on the course of action they will take. Luzie lies awake in her mother's arms. Sybille is surprised she is willing to leave and not argue that they should stay and give the man another chance at explaining himself, to find out his true motives. They agree that only Sybille will move around in the dark, packing three bags, all of which were lying half-full of essentials in the front room by the door anyway, in case of an emergency. He left the torch as wordless guarantee downstairs and she will take that too. They will leave within the hour before he awakes from his first sleep. They will walk the horse to the railroad and mount it there. Sybille, the more experienced rider, will take the reigns. When she asks which direction they will take – east or west – and Hilda does not answer, Sybille understands that the real argument will take place in the dark of night, far from the man and the compound.

Luzie is asleep by the time it is ready to go and her grandmother breathes on her eyes and strokes her face wordlessly to rouse her. Sybille moves slowly, tying her daughter's shoes somnolently as she thinks how desperate they are that they are leaving the one connection to William that they have. Setting out again after this year of permanence, like they did so many times before, only this time without William. The sadness makes it hard to breathe. She tells herself: The man talked of rape; he was lying about being William's friend. William doesn't have friends. In any case, leaving him here and taking his horse means they have a chance to find William. No matter how unlikely, it is better than any alternative she can conjure. Perhaps, one day, they can come back.

Sybille puts the torch in her jacket pocket and follows the other two figures out the door.

Outside, the wind has died down and the sky is clear and the world a dull set of shapes, leaden and quiet. Like a jealous lover, she imagines what this man has done to William to extract the knowledge he has about them: she sees for a few seconds a torture scene in her mind as they cross the courtyard, the man fixed on breaking bones, pulling nails, strangulation. William never speaks about Sybille and their relationship to other people: since the beginning, he had acted like she was his little secret. Such decorum and discretion she found bizarre and loveable in a man who was in many ways very strange. At turns it had made her angry, when it seemed as if he was embarrassed by her or their couple-dom somehow. Then she grew used to it.

Suddenly, she stops. And she reaches a hand out to hold her mother up too.

— I forgot my book. And my notebook. I have to go back for them.

She can't believe that she was almost about to leave behind the two things that keep her united to the world beyond base survival. Both items are upstairs, not in the room the man is sleeping in but in her room next door.

— Our past is in that notebook, she whispers, sensing her mother's desperate disagreement. It's all I have now. I won't be a minute. It's ok. Just wait for me here.

Placing her backpack at the feet of her mother and her daughter, there in the middle of the courtyard, she scampers back to the house, untying her boots and slipping out of them before quietly opening the back door and entering the house.

She breathes a moment or two once inside and listens and tells herself she hears the faint sound of the man asleep. Moving quickly and silently, she goes through the front room into the hall and starts to ascend the stairs, pausing at the turn before moving extra quietly up the last flight and then straight and fluid through to her room. In the dark she has to trust her memory and not succumb to the need for balance or for touch assurance.

The book she finds by the bed where she guessed it to be: battered and dogeared, its black weight a deeply familiar comfort. Below the bed is the notebook. And now she is back out in the hall, passing the door beyond which lies the sleeping man whose snoring has ceased so that she imagines him awake and waiting to spring out and grab her.

On the last step of the stairs before the turn, she misjudges: instead of stepping into space she steps onto floor, stumbling and bumping into the wall. The disturbance seems to stir the house itself as she breathes in between her blood throbbing through her head, convinced she heard the man move in his bed. Now she is taking the rest of the stairs as if it's midday – the sounds of the world are at full volume. By the door she is sure she hears him rise and get up from the bed and she bends to grab her shoes from where they sit beside the basin – she threw it there when this calamity first befell – and she puts them up under the crook of her arm as she runs towards her family, hissing:

— Let's go, let's go, let's go! itself spoken in acceleration so that the words gel together and, tilting with speed and hands held as a chain, the three rush toward the laneway. Feared noise emanates from the house, their fallen sanctuary. Pursuit as feeling, vibration in the night air. But the horse is still standing where they last came upon it. And after a frantic search, Sybille finds the lasso and frees it from the gatepost.

— Go on, get up. Luzie wait, I'll help you up once mormor is up.

The horse is awake and breathing in bursts through its nostrils and drawing out in an agitated dance a small revolution across the lane. Finally Hilda and Luzie are up and Sybille, juggling the two boots, the book and notebook as well as the reins manages to hoist herself up, though kicking her mother in the stomach as she straddles the beast and dropping one of her boots.

— Hey! Wait! Stop! comes from behind them. The man is running at a sprint out of the courtyard and Sybille digs her heels into the horse's flank and she curses the loss of the boot for the worse possible loss is always footwear and the horse is galloping down the narrow strait of the lane with low lying branches hitting their faces.

— Sons of bitches! You will never find him.

Luzie looks over her shoulder terrified and sees the figure of the man running though failing to keep up and slowly he disappears into the dark of the night like the ravelled edges of a waking nightmare.

Burley Fisher Books

FOR READERS
BY WRITERS

400 Kingsland Road, E8 4AA
shop@burleyfisherbooks.com
020 7249 2263

CLAIM YOUR FREE
£5 NATIONAL BOOK TOKEN

This voucher entitles you to a free gift from your bookseller!

Just visit the below link, or scan the QR code, and enter your unique code. We'll send your £5 e-Gift card by email the next day, so you can take it back to your local bookshop to spend on more books.*

nationalbooktokens.com/highfive

Your unique code: PSJWHVCF

Claim your National Book Tokens e-Gift card by 31st January 2025

Initial Value
£5.00

NATIONAL BOOK TOKENS

Card number:
1234 5678 9012 3456 789
PIN
123

High Five from your local independent bookshop to you!

ook Tokens have been giving booklovers what they want since 1932. For the sixth year, we're giving **of thousands of free e-Gift cards** to celebrate independent bookshops and the people who shop in them. ve to your lovely local bookshop – and **high five** to you for supporting them!

NATIONAL BOOK tokens

WE ♥ INDEPENDENT BOOKSHOPS

discover National Book Tokens Discover helps you take your National Book Tokens experience even further; it's your ultimate destination for all things books, brought to you by the nation's favourite gift for booklovers. Don't miss out – sign up today to discover what's going on at your local bookshop, as well as our book recommendations, competitions and quizzes, all delivered straight to your inbox.

Plus: every month we'll enter you to win a £100 National Book Token!

nationalbooktokens.com/discover

*1. Your free £5 National Book Token will be sent to you by email as a National Book Tokens e-Gift card. 2. Your National Book Tokens e-Gift card must be claimed by 23:59 on Friday 31st January 2025. After this date, you will no longer be able to claim and your unique code will be null and void. 3. Your e-Gift card will be sent to the email address you provide the day after your online claim, providing the claim is valid. 4. This offer is available to customers aged 16 and above and is limited to one £5 e-Gift card per person and per valid email address; no cash alternative will be offered. 5. Employees of Book Tokens Ltd, the Booksellers Association and participating bookshops are not eligible to claim a free e-Gift card. For full terms and conditions, please visit nationalbooktokens.com/highfive

O to sing of the freedom from the horse! The great uncou-
pling from nature, from whence you start to see yourself
apart from other animals and plants, the great world-tree
even. The end begins in the year 1814 when James Watt
puts the power of steam to industrial use and look ahead
and you shall see the extraction of coal, millennia of com-
pressed effort, burned and released as carbon, the slow
smothering of the world-tree by what is – always – lost in
the creation of anything.

See a man down a mineshaft, George Stephenson, fix-
ing a broken water pump. The father of the railway. Also
that of a son called Robert.

In the year 1825 the Stockton and Darlington Railway
opens, a complete package of steam engine, wheels and
tracks, this is the birth of the world-machine itself. The

dreams of horses and canals alike are sated. Four years further along and the industrial hearts of Liverpool and Manchester are to be connected by rail, with The Rocket locomotive, the fastest thing a human had ever set eyes on, moving at fifty kilometres per hour. Time is now winning over space. Do you know what that means? The race has started: iron tracks spread out and grow from this perfidious start. Church bells are no longer the arbiters of time and so the world gets Railroad Time, uniform and regular acceleration demands temporal exactitude in far flung locations simultaneously. The casualness of natural steps, of we'll see each other when we see each other, no longer suffices.

Can anybody hear us?

We're saying that by the year 1835 the first tracks are laid in Germany – the land you now call Germany – the Bavarian Ludwig Railway is the first installment in the cataclysmic German Train Network.

The forest sighs with its sleepers and flies continue to buzz furiously against the deception of windows.

The first German train is British designed and called The Adler. By the year 1859 the river Rhine is conquered at Cologne with the great Cathedral Bridge, which now plugs into what is becoming the West European Rail Network. The continent is becoming interconnected.

Some networks come into existence by royal decree of fat kings, others to move people such as in Belgium and Germany, others still to move goods, material, facilitate capital intercourse. But what all these new systems share is that they draw people together, uniting countries and the lands upon which they spread. The nation state, the troublemaker for the coming century, is right up ahead. Every decision is important: the French rail network is in government hands from the beginning, while the Anglo-Saxon favours private enterprise, creating barons and monopolies. Tentacles reach cities such as Paris, deepening its centrifugal force as an epicentre, while in Germany the tracks are decentered, running every which way like water filling the decks of a slowly sinking ship. These machines bellow through vale and town at the astonishing speed of eighty kilometres an hour, such vitesse elevating and shaking down society to its very core. The paperback novel, a comfortable spring loaded chair. The beach lies singing too, waiting to be explored.

The first military conflict fed by trains sees the French and Prussians transport their men by carriage locomotive. It is the year 1870 and the machine dresses up the brutal barbarity of war in new vestments, which helps in the telling of the tale of progress and civility. Black smoke, drunkenness and madness. The future is here and it rushes in great billows of sooty air through the darkened night, soldiers singing as resolute cannon fodder. We plough on mercilessly.

CHAPTER VII

When they finally approach Öresund Bridge, on an afternoon in late spring, they are relieved to see the huge bridge is still intact, still rising out of the water between the two lands. To leave Sweden is such a milestone. And though the days are growing longer, they are still short. They waste no time in getting onto the bridge, bypassing Malmö by going around it to the north.

Tendrils and dirty scarfs of smoke show that people still reside in its centre. They haven't seen all that many people since leaving Oslo a month before. The whole way, they have been avoiding towns and cities, surviving on the food they have brought with them, only daring to go toward a building when they need water and are not near a stream or a lake. Anytime they did see people before, they have always scrambled to get out of view.

If it was obvious they were already spotted, they hurried as quickly as they could off the road and away from whoever it was coming along, checking to make sure they weren't pursuing them.

The exception was Gothenburg, where Luzie was born five years before. There they travelled into the centre spurred on more by curiosity and a little sentimentality than anything else. They visited the main road exit south of the city to see if there were any messages pertaining to them or to their friends Dea and Trygve. Roadside billboards such as these, along with the rough broadsides printed by often deranged groups in ownership of an old hand press, were often to be found in toll booths or some protected gateway or other, forms of communication that were both rudimentary and unreliable. They had found nothing related to them or anybody they knew.

They walk onto the massive bridge as the evening's wan light starts to fade. Sybille guesses that William is doing maths in his head, adding days to years to calculate a figure that represents the passing of life in darktime. He often announces a number in the evening, a tally in which Sybille finds a weird, uneasy pride. When Sybille and William made the journey in the opposite direction five years before, they had run across the bridge fighting strong wind currents. Now the world has grown into itself, with fewer humans and even less of their electricity. The bridge itself looks like an unnatural protrusion liable to buckle and collapse, one more scar of humanity.

— I'm not sure there are people on the bridge, William says to Sybille when they are out of earshot of Hilda and Luzie, but who knows?

— Let's see, Sybille says flatly, we could be walking straight into a trap.

The lanes in both directions are filled with cars and many are burned out. Some contain skeletons, while others seem once to have been turned into campsites, makeshift abodes, since abandoned. All the signs of the pandemonium in the immediate hours and days after the darkening lay wasted and forlorn. Sybille looks out into the channel and sees the tall stalks of the wind turbines lined up in rows of geometrical formality, broken by the odd fallen fan or bole as the wind farm slowly collapses into the sea under its own weight and redundancy. These structures are moaning to each other out in the growing dark. Sybille grows suddenly scared, their progress across the bridge too slow because they have to weave a way through the car wreckages and dross. She picks up her pace then. And Hilda notices her picking up her pace and, taking Luzie's hand, matches the faster pace. So in turn Luzie picks up the scent and the fear of eyes prying comes upon her and she squeezes her grandmother's hand.

— What is it? Hilda tries to keep her voice calm. Sybille? William? What is it?

By now, all of them are jogging and breathing heavy and salty wind soughs through the stanchions of the massive structure itself, so long one can't see one end from the other and they have yet to reach even its midpoint.

The further along it they move the more it feels like the bridge itself might give out and topple into the deep and salty water below. With the fading light of day, danger is now pervasive and intractable and they are fully enveloped within it. The soughing sound is almost deafening as the dark of night settles in and they are running silently as a group now, but no attack comes and eventually they reach the Danish side. There, the bridge is abandoned and empty of living people, only unburied piles of bones and supine skeletons lay any claim to it.

The sun cuts the scene in two: half of the world laying in shadow while the rest bathes in the yellow light of summer. The four of them sit in the stand of a former town-edge stadium with leaves and rubbish slowly moving across the erstwhile pitch, stirred by a light breeze. All that's left are uneven mounds of accumulated years of leaf-mould. They have been on the move for a number of weeks and are feeling tired yet restless. To cross the continent was an undertaking decided upon in penury. Another winter in Oslo would have killed them.

— We can rest a bit more and then move on.
— I'm tired.
— We're all tired.

They get up and slowly move through the tiered stadium seats. Advertising boarding hangs down from the second storey seating area. A collapsed floodlight in the near corner extends out into the pitch it had once lit. Sybille jogs ahead, then jumps down into the tunnel that leads below the stands to the changing rooms to see if there is any salvage. Everything is trashed and in disarray from a sort of makeshift triage influenza centre. In the main tunnel-network, leaves of recent years run along the walls, the concrete creating damp mulch and below this organic matter lies towels and blankets and buckets. In the inner rooms lie bones from the make-shift morgue. No salvage, not even a vending machine for which she realises she had been subconsciously searching. She leaves and retraces her steps and exits the tunnel out into the field and passes out under the shadow of the stand into the light. She is momentarily dazzled and closes her eyes, and tries to imagine the scene on matchday. But Luzie is calling her from up in the corner of the stand somewhere and so she opens her eyes and laughs, waves her arms.

— I'm coming!

They leave the town with the football stadium in early afternoon, just as the heat really asserts itself. They have one of those talks they sometimes have about what wholesale disaster and catastrophe were like before the darkening, in the space of a collective imagination or in works of art, in books and film. Hilda's take on it is the most benign: these things happen, they have always happened. There is no comparison to make for it is always relative: famine, pandemic, genocide, war. They have always been there but sometimes they just affected some and not others. And now it is everyone's time.

William remembers how people would revel in the spectacle of catastrophe collectively, fed in the last years by social and news media. Being housebound due to blizzards or the tailend of a hurricane gave a sense of unity to the atomised world of modern, electric living. Sybille just remembers the anxiety that nothing was remaining the same and the sense of impending disaster that was irrevocable: the hand wringing of her teenage years, her twenties, in the face of climate change and the obvious myopia of oil extraction, degradation, fossils fuelling a species bent on destroying its only habitat. The burning of wildfires. Drought. Mountains of plastic waste.

Such conversations are for the benefit of Luzie, some kind of misguided effort of education and anamnesis, an effort to keep alive the memory across the generations of how it once was. They often make them laugh and smile because the memories of these works of art so concerned with disaster and catastrophe appear absurd and slightly silly in the face of their present lived reality.

Sybille asks: Why were there always mounds of burning animals at the start of movies? There were always heaps of burning horses or cows with their legs stuck up in the air. What did it mean?

— I guess it was meant to signify efforts at stopping the spread of disease, William tries to reason. From all the dead livestock left when there was nobody left to man the farms.

— I have never seen any burning mounds of horses, Hilda adds.

— Well you spent the early days in Oslo. I think it was

calmer. I mean within minutes I was carrying a dead body.

— Perhaps, Hilda says, I did have an easy introduction to the chaos.

— We saw some big bonfires on our way to the coast after Berlin. Didn't we Sybille? Some of them were huge.

— Yeah I forgot about them. Huge fires. It's so long ago now.

This town, like so many others, is nothing more than a collection of buildings that now just sits out in the land, slowly crumbling and being taken over by nature, with nothing more than the occasional odd figure slowly stepping around it. A little later they are in the flat open country to the town's south. They plan to keep moving with unhurried defilade until the afternoon has burned itself out and they can pitch their tent behind as much cover as possible.

— We can still probably speak to people in Danish here, Hilda says to Sybille, but perhaps we will need some German.

— How is your German? Soon there won't be any more Danish.

— My German is good enough. I think.

— Should we speak English?

— I don't see what speaking English will give us, Hilda says, if they're older people we shouldn't speak English at all. That's just my opinion.

— We speak to communicate.

— But people don't want to speak to strangers, Sybille says, English marks us as strangers.

— Okay we can try in German, even though bad and accented German is just the same as English.

Each has a salvaged backpack and across the four bags their earthly goods are distributed. William carries an axe in his hand. In winter he used it almost daily for wood but in summer it is more a talisman than tool. Sybille carries a squat five litre plastic container of water they last filled the morning before from the water tank in the attic of a low house on land that had been formerly designated Denmark. Hilda carries the lamp but they have no oil for it since before the last full moon.

They mostly speak English among themselves and William shows that he appreciates this but Sybille feels it to be some atavism that puts him at the head of the family. Of course she speaks Norwegian with Hilda but they aren't often alone. Luzie is losing a claim to either language day by day and finding this disturbing, Sybille searches in the face of William to see if he shares her feelings, but she sees nothing. She can only worry now as they walk further south into German speaking territory that there can be no union here: at the very least brief exchanges she reckons but probably more likely outright hostility. This is a disadvantage for them all and none more than for the girl. Much of what is left to say are expressions of need and beyond that the outlining of what has been lost but Luzie doesn't even have that.

The land before them is quiet and mostly empty and they move down the autobahn quickly enough, passing the odd shell of a car and broken tarmac issuing saplings or flowers, the verge having long ago taken over. It is mid-afternoon and a good time to seek a place to camp for the night and to look for any salvage and so they veer off the autobahn at a point where a bridge crosses it. They scramble up the embankment and join the small road heading toward a church spire and a cluster of roofs gathered around it. At the town-edge sits a petrol station.

— Hold up, says William, let's take a rest. I'll check the pumps.

They silently follow his lead, setting down their individual loads and sitting heavily on the curb of the trashed station, enjoying the shade and momentary respite. There is nothing in the pumps so he goes to inspect the reservoir tank beneath the apron: the manhole was removed long ago and he can't spot it anywhere in the vicinity. He lies down and lowers his head into the echoeful gloom and sniffs and smells only damp and the faintest memory of the scent of petroleum but perhaps he is imagining even that.

The women haven't moved from where they sit. He walks by them and into the building. Sybille follows. Everything is trashed and organic matter reaches into the back rooms where the windows have given out and welcomed in leaves, the seeds of grasses, ivy fingers. Someone lived there for a time. They can tell by the patterns of the stains around a makeshift bed, a well worn path to and from the corner out through the store, a small accumulation of books by the head of the bed. They are textbooks of some sort. Economics, computer programming. In the far corner a fireplace for when it got too cold. The wall skudded black in a conical spray of soot and smoke.

— Nothing here, he says and Sybille just nods wordlessly.

— You think it snows here in winter? Sybille asks nobody in particular when they are back outside.

— It snows everywhere Sybille, William says.

She can't remember when she became the one among them to constantly hope for a home and he became the one set on going as far south as they physically could.

— We have to keep moving, we haven't even left the north yet.

— I know, I know. I'm just... She doesn't continue the conversation and instead walks back outside where she picks up a stone and essays to lob it clean into the manhole where it lays like a black void in the bright sunshine. The stone passes through the middle of the hole and disappears below silently. It's just I'm trying to calculate the distances. Timing. I mean, we're already tired.

— Well Sybille, Hilda says, we will keep going because we have to.

Sybille frowns at this as it adds nothing to the conversation as far as she can see, her mother always trying too hard in her eyes to be a neutral arbiter between them.

— Let's go, let's head into the town.

They pick themselves up and don their backpacks and move out onto the town's road. The air is still, birds calling to each other the only sound. It is very hot. They are on the main street and approaching the small rise on which the church sits when they hear a call and they all turn and look back the way they have come to spot the figure approaching. An older, rotund man with a head of white hair who holds nothing in his hands and waves once he sees he has their attention. They have stopped as a group and William grips the axe in his hand and his eyes move rapidly, taking in the buildings up and down the street. They can hear the man's breathing, heavy and short and unhealthy, from twenty metres away.

— Hallo, he says cheerfully in German.

— Hello, William speaks back in English. The man is all smiles and surprises them by offering his hand, shaking each in turn from eldest to youngest.

— We're just passing through, Hilda says.

— Yes, people often do. You're welcome. We don't have much. Just my wife and I here now, there are some people in the east of the town but don't go to them. Avoid, yes. Our sons also went west at the start of last summer.

He is well kept despite his unhealthy state: his beard is neat, his hair also. He has on a button-down shirt that is clean, shirt sleeves rolled as if he is coming from the office. His belly bulges vigorously above his canvas trousers and seems like it is threatening to pop at any moment: he eats well, it is clear. Has done for quite some time.

— They have gone toward the electricity, he continues.

We didn't want to go, we have everything we need here to live out the end of our days. Have you heard about the electricity in the west?

His demeanour changes and from one moment to the next he is more serious. The group of four look at each other: Luzie frowns and is about to ask her mother a question when the grandmother speaks:

— No, what do you mean by electricity? There is no electricity anymore. She speaks like she would to Luzie, with the same soft and flat tone that allows for the existence of multiple other possibilities but all of them being wrong save the one she just offered.

The man just laughs and then says:

— Well of course but around a year ago, maybe more, people started to pass through here and speak about electricity as if it were fact. The first people we thought to be crazy, religious fanatics maybe or tricksters. But our two sons went south. To look for friends and to trade, down near Hanover and there they heard the same.

— Wait, what? William interjects in English. What type of electricity, how?

Hilda translates as best she can and excitement spreads between them as the large white-haired man smiles and nods his head vigorously as if the act of translation itself verifies the rumours.

— Where are you from? he asks William, speaking the English words hesitantly but fluently.

— Where is anyone from, William says a little histrionically, raising his arms up in supplication before slapping his sides gently. I grew up on the island of Ireland.

— Ah! I've been there once, the man says triumphantly, yes, I went as a tourist. He says this sheepishly but then laughs and everyone smiles with the exception of Luzie.

— Wait, but the electricity: where is it exactly and who managed to create it?

— I do not know. To the west. Not Germans, perhaps French. My wife and I. Our two sons left and will come back. Electricity … It exists again … He is stammering and unable to put sentences together in English and doesn't like this disability. He grows quiet and Sybille wonders if maybe he doesn't want to tell these strangers too much and she thinks she sees the man's demeanour change: now that he has told them his exciting news it is as if he has no more time for them.

— Have you much food here? Sybille asks baldly.

— No. He says this simply as if her blunt question deserves nothing less than the obvious answer. He shakes his head, then absentmindedly pats his belly, in a way that seems to Sybille to be an obscene gesture and he looks at them each in turn as if to ask if they have any other idiotic questions and that if not then the conversation was going to end.

— Good, he says switching back to German, you are welcome to pass the night here but please do not outstay your welcome and leave us in peace.

Hilda starts to summarise and the man smiles and turns to leave before stopping and pointing at William: Ireland was a beautiful place. Truly. The Ring of Kerry. The Book of Kells. I'm sorry you cannot go back there.

Sybille thinks: Even now, here, you only talk to the man, ask where he is from and console him. Men really are their own country.

That evening they pitch camp on the edge of the town, as far away as possible from the church and its grass that seems so soft and well kept. The town appears to be deserted other than the strange white-haired Santa man. Sybille and William sit up late, past sunset, looking out over the field that stretches below them, quietly talking as the other two fall asleep in the tent after a brief bedtime story.

— What do you make of it?

— I don't know: it always seemed possible that electricity would return, but obviously it's not much more than rumour.

— Or demented hope.

— That also. He lost his sons to the rumour so of course he tells himself it is true.

— They probably have just left him. Some people just can't stay put.

— It's definitely intriguing though, don't you think?

— I can't help but be sceptical. But yes, I think it's worth our while to ask anybody we come across if they've heard of electricity.

— Not everyone we come across will be like this man. We are risking our lives travelling the way we are.

— Yes but our lives are over if we don't move. There is no more food anywhere. And in winter we will simply freeze to death.

— I know, I know but let's just keep it in mind. Besides, the west. France is not as cold as here.

This conversation, like so many before, goes on for a long time, often in circles, speaking as they both are from positions of ignorance, conjecture. At some point he puts a hand on her thigh and she ignores it before finally moving her leg entirely and his hand falls to the ground.

In the days that follow they develop a routine and rhythm that sees them rise just before daybreak and disband their bivouac and be on their way by dawn in order to cover as many kilometres as possible before the sun rises so high in the sky it becomes too hot to move comfortably. People can be spotted out in the landscape slowly moving, tending crops or moving carts or directing drayhorses, members of farms run by collectives big and small that had absolutely no interest in strangers such as themselves. They make sure to stay clear of them, for the risk of being run off lands across boundaries invisible or dangerous or worse being shot at or having dogs set upon them. One late afternoon they hear the loud crack of gunfire, four shots in quick succession and have no way of telling if the target was man or beast or the air itself.

It is Sybille who discovers the vegetable garden, walking a back lane to urinate. It's at the back of a townhouse, and has recently been tended. The beds are weeded and tilled and at the back in the wall-corner lies a heap of freshly cut vines.

She goes through the house shouting a greeting and when no response comes she goes out the front door into the town's mainstreet and calls the group to come back. They file through the house, where they find signs of occupation but no victuals or bedding. In the high-walled garden, they put down their backpacks and Hilda starts to harvest the peas and tomatoes without uttering a word. William watches her and frowns but doesn't question her. Sybille wishes she would have refrained in front of Luzie but what did it matter she tells herself, they are desperate.

They camp in the town and after three days nobody shows up. Sybille takes it as a sign:

— People are leaving, after all this time and even in the middle of summer.

— But where do you think they're going, asks Hilda, why would you leave a garden you've been tending all spring?

— I don't know, William shakes his head and looks up into the sky, I don't know what it means and it certainly doesn't suggest we should think they've gone far. Or forever.

Now on the third day of being in the town they do an inventory of their food. It isn't much: two tins of tuna, and the bounty from the garden, which amounts to tomatoes and beans enough for a couple of meals only.

— This is why it's not going to be possible to keep moving forever. Four mouths is too many mouths to feed from salvage alone.

— I know Sybille, don't think I don't get it, but there's no point shoring up in a place for winter just to die there slowly with hunger. As William speaks, he shoves items back into the backpack.

Sybille turns around and walks some steps away, breathing heavily and looks up at the wildflowers and birch trees running along the stonewall. Winter is a certainty. Luzie is chasing a butterfly. One of so few. Insects went with circuitry and that's when the food really started to run out: their job now is to chase and hunt whatever they can.

— We should get going, Sybille says and starts to move then stops and turns saying: But William.

He looks up at her after a beat.

— What?

— Promise me we will stop moving by the end of autumn.

— End of autumn? Sure. Before then even. Winter's going to be real.

— Before autumn? Well then maybe let's stay a while here?

The garden is an idyllic scene just then: their daughter dancing under the flitting flight of a butterfly, Hilda kneeling as she moves her hands through vines, a sense of stilled calm.

— Okay then, let's stay here. We can see how it goes.

— Thank you. Sybille turns from the house door and moves to him, kissing him briefly on the lips. Thank you. It's the right thing to do.

— But we can't stay in this house. The people who tended this vegetable garden could come back at any moment. Let's go find another house.

They leave Luzie with her grandmother and pass through almost every house in the town, which William declares to have been more a village technically speaking. Sybille tries to imagine the lives lived there, the scenes played out and not just in the time immediately before the darkening but throughout history, in the time of horses, serfdom. The time before electricity. The main street runs in a looping Z shape so that one approaches from the side before turning down onto the main drag of the village, and then swinging left to exit out onto the surrounding open fields.

They find a suitable house at the far end of the town, one of the last houses before the town runs out of itself. It is bigger than many others and has a pleasant garden that is about to bloom. The occupants had children Luzie's age and there are a number of toys she finds to play with in her own way.

The owners of the vegetable garden never do return, and neither does anybody else reveal themselves: they have the village to themselves. Hilda and Sybille spend a lot of time in the vegetable garden, tilling it and admiring the plants and flowers. William moves about on his own, spending the days inspecting houses and trying to understand the town and its history and Sybille can see that his mind is looking for answers to the most obscure questions, such as why this town exists at all or when exactly each of the buildings were built. In the evenings he talks about the system of vassalage and tithes that governed the land in the last dark age. Or how many young men died in the First and Second World Wars and where the sewage had gone to be treated and how many litres of water the reservoir can hold and why the transistor station for the electrical grid was located where it was.

Sybille tries to write in her notebook but finds she can't concentrate for any meaningful amount of time. She finds herself staring at the page for an unknown amount of minutes, unable to finish her sentence:

William brought up David again, going back over where he could have been the day of the darkening. I can see his mind picking up the puzzle again. The puzzle being

One afternoon, William and Sybille sit at the bank by the water reservoir. It is a windy, cloudy day and warm in a way that suggests thunder. Sybille is in no mood to argue. Then suddenly William speaks, as if he has been holding the words back for a while and the stillness of the reservoir gives him the push to say what he wants to say.

— He had gone off the rails, he starts, apropos of nothing in particular, as far as Sybille can see and she almost laughs at how dramatic he sounds.

— He had gone off the rails and there was nothing his teachers or our parents could do, William says solemnly.

He is talking about his brother David.

— Sounds like me at that age, Sybille says, forcing a levity she doesn't feel.

— I think he wanted me to prove that I cared about him, William continues and Sybille feels a pinch of sympathy for his loss. Still, she can't help frowning.

— By forcing you to help him? She is no longer sure where the conversation is going.

— We complement each other in that way. David is outgoing and vivacious while I'm more of an introvert. I mean, you know this. He always made wrong decisions at his own expense in order to please other people who don't really give a shit one way or another about him. He was always off smoking cigarettes at school with older guys, or drinking booze in parks with all sorts of people.

— A generous weakness, perhaps, adds Sybille though she immediately regrets saying it: as an only child she has no siblings to discuss with William and finds it hard to imagine the defensive impulse to protect or deflect on a sibling's behalf. He doesn't reply and soon he gets up, starts walking back towards the garden where Hilda and Luzie are waiting for them. Wordlessly, she joins him.

That evening they discuss their plans once more. William argues that staying stationary will lead to hunger and possibly to attack. But the others convey how travelling incessantly will lead to the mendacity of nomadism and vulnerability of simple bad luck. They get out the map once more and William moves his dirty finger over it and calculates distances in terms of the energy of Luzie and Hilda.

— I think we should go west where winters are less severe.

Sybille stares at his dirty forefinger and imagines the arcs it is making in his mind.

— Don't worry William, you're right, we should keep going west.

William wants to be alone and so spends the days alone. He sets snares and other traps for any animals that might be around the town and nearby countryside and is lucky on the first day but not subsequent. He gathers firewood and delivers it to the back of their house then spends the rest of each day at the bank by the reservoir, staring into its surface slick with bloom and fallen debris, a mute lake that somewhat terrifies him. His station above it, behind the steel handrail, gives him a static strength and he tells himself: you're not going to jump into it so stop thinking that you will jump into it.

Once when he's carrying a load of branchfall from the reservoir he hears dogs before he sees them, a low pitched series of growls and whelps. As he turns the corner onto the mainstreet he sees to his right, in a corner between house and townwall, a gaggle of black forms tearing at something between them. He stops short and as he does so their collective attention turns to him and as one of the dogs lets out a garrulous bark the rest start to run at him. He remembers in this instant his friend John telling him as they walked along a country road in Ireland, passing a bungalow with a dog barking wildly: the only thing to do in the face of a pack of wild dogs is to get down on the ground, that way you show that you've submitted to their dominance. And so like a true fool or desperate penitent he throws the branchfall and axe to the side of him just as they close down the distance and he jumps to the tarmac with his hands under his chest. He lets out a wail then, his only concession to the pure fear pumping adrenaline through his body and then the dogs are upon him and as he feels the teeth of one down his side he jumps up kicking so that one of the four goes flying in the air and the rest are up on their hind quarters as if making a lunge for his neck and somehow he gets his axe even as one sinks their teeth into his forearm and he starts to flail with it.

He connects with one black mongrel and it goes to ground with a warm crack. This sets the others back a moment enough to allow him to swing and connect with another so that a hesitation sets in amongst their frenzy. He starts to back away from the remaining two as he poises the axe in the air. He looks over to where they were and sees that they had been working over a long dried up carcass of what he guesses to be a cow and sees then how emaciated they are. And weak. One is barking incessantly in fury and the other starts to do a circle, skittish and distracted and not knowing what it wants to do other than to eat something and survive.

— They're not like the dogs we knew before, he says as Sybille washes his bite-wound, in the parlour of the house they are staying in. They've reverted to wildness. And they're hungry like us. Crazed. Wolves basically.

— We have to be so much more careful. Dogs, I never would have thought that dogs would become a threat.

— Ah! he winces.

— Sorry, I'm almost done.

He has a total of five bite-wounds on his arms and

down his left side and around both his ankles. Hilda and Luzie look on concerned.

— It's things like this that will kill us, you know.

— Oh please, don't say that, Hilda says and pulls Luzie closer to her.

— But Hilda, it's true. We need to be aware of that, William is as measured and calm as he possibly can be, we don't have much more antibiotics. Some of the contents of our medkit is from when Luzie was born! We don't even know if it still works.

— Why? What's wrong with when I was born? The girl whines and wriggles in her grandmother's embrace, indignant.

— Nothing honey, it's just a long time because you're a grown up now, and William smiles at his daughter and Sybille realises it's the first time he has smiled in a very long time.

— So you don't think they had rabies do you? Sybille asks as she starts to apply the bandages of torn strips of linen.

— How many times. No, I think they were just crazed with hunger. At least we can only hope. But if I start to get sick tonight I should probably take some antibiotics and we can stay here in case I have a fever or whatever. Even though I really want to move.

— We will move, don't worry, she says simply. Also as a doctor I should probably tell you that you don't survive rabies.

Though Sybille smiles, she's disturbed by William's unsmiling manner, and the constant talk of his brother.

She lies awake that night, waiting for his temperature to go up or for his limbs to start to seize up but he falls sound asleep before long. Nothing stirs except her mind until finally, hours after the others do, she slips off into a restless sleep. She dreams of underwater exploration and William's previous life hunting the crust of the earth along the seabed and the points of extraction for the oil that lays below it. The dream takes place not in the brightly lit rooms with computer screens with graphs and spreadsheets of how it had been, but instead in the murky gloom of the ocean and she is diving with William who holds his axe and who is communicating in Norwegian, though not to her, to someone else, somewhere above them, probably on a floating oilrig and she realises he is searching for the point in the seabed that will give them access to what they want – light and electricity. Then the dream digresses and a succubus comes at her with its fangs showing and barks in the black water, huge air bubbles bulging furiously from its mouth. But Sybille isn't afraid. William cuts the dog down and goes onwards to the point from which light is shining and sticks an arm through and then his head and soon he has squeezed into this new world of light and electricity and she follows and it is dry and William is standing tall and laughing.

Soon the death-dogs force them to leave the town. It is Luzie who coined the term dødhund: death-dogs. Black forms that move in a formation of panicked chaos. In the space of five years humans lost their preeminence in the natural world. Now this pack circles the town and threatens the little respite they found there.

They decamp well before the sun reaches its zenith and wordlessly leave the house that was home for a couple of weeks, the longest since leaving Oslo. There is relief in the fact that William seems fine, just sore along his wounds. He even goes by himself to fill their water bottles, dismissing their fear that more dødhunds could be laying in wait. But when he comes back he appears in a rush and speaks as if he is angry:

— I think we should avoid staying in small towns like this.

— Okay, perhaps you're right.

— Either we find a community or we make our own community in some farm somewhere. Somewhere self-sufficient.

— I guess. Sybille hesitates, looks at her mother. A farm sounds good.

On the way out of town they pass the war memorial to those fallen in the wars of the century previous and without noticing or speaking a word William steps out of line and crosses their path and swings his axe at the stone plinth and with the impact he releases his hold on the shaft. A spark or two issues as a tiny chip asserts itself with an empty twang of uncomfortable metal. The tool falls to the ground. Sybille draws Luzie closer to her.

— William … What?

He reaches down with his head lowered and retrieves the axe and inspects its head and then turns and spits

83

forcefully to where the axe made contact as if the stela is a thing of disgust and had insulted them all.

— Well that is one way to say goodbye, Sybille says brightly to Luzie, an effort to deflect, and hide her own fright. The girl remains silent, doesn't respond. William continues down the road as if nothing amiss took place. Sybille looks to her mother, but Hilda just starts walking after him, her face set in a tight neutral expression.

They continue south each day, usually making between twenty and thirty kilometres before it's time to set up camp. Often they leave roads behind them and cut across land, directed toward a point on the map William set upon in the morning. More than once they have to retreat due to impassable hedgerows. Luzie, Hilda and the need to acquire food slow them down and every evening Sybille finds a moment to whisper quietly to William that there is no rush and that there is no point running south just to starve somewhere else all the same. It's an impossible situation she concedes, but they're exhausted. He nods his head silently but she knows he's going to suggest the next morning that they keep moving all the same.

— Luzie, come here to your daddy, he says one evening just before they are about to turn in. Come and give your daddy a hug. And the child dutifully goes to him where he sits cross legged on the ground and receives his hug mindlessly and squirms into his lap.

— The only puzzle we have to solve is to keep you safe, isn't that right my dear?

— Yes, the girl says, and puckers out her lips toward the dying embers of their fire. And mama and mormor and you too. We all have to be safe.

— Everyone is safe and tomorrow will always be better than yesterday. Wait until you see.

— In tomorrow will be better than in yesterday?

— Yup, that's right.

They are always aiming for rivers because William feels that rivers and water can give the easiest protection and an obvious source of water and potentially food. But it is hard to follow the rivers in places and the first two they try to follow they give up on. It took all their energy as they spent fruitless hours walking to navigate their meandering course. The banks are populated in places by bands of people all with the same idea: they see at least two rudimentary watermills being worked to power various activities. One day, William approaches a settlement, axeless and the three others a safe distance out of sight, but the three men he encounters shake their heads when he starts to speak English and pretty quickly start speaking in German or Friesian or some language that sounds runic and bygone. Whatever it is, it is clear they are telling him to leave. William begs, pleads, sure that they had to understand him, English had been common before the darkening. He rubs his stomach, mimicked pregnancy, marks the height of a child. Pointing back the way he had come as if behind him he has an army of women and children in need and at death's door. But even in doing this, he sees what they see: a stranger, a skinny, dark-eyed, lank haired tramp with filthy clothes speaking a language not their own.

The people in the second camp raise knives and throw stones, forcing him to flee.

Luzie is often the first to wake, and when she does she slips out of the tent as quietly as possible, sometimes it takes a full ten minutes of pulling at the zip so slowly in order for it not to make a sound. Her efforts are more often than not in vain for her parents stir with her first movement and then watch the small frame of their daughter backlit against the green glow of the tent's canvas slowly being lit by the rising sun. It breaks Sybille's heart that her daughter's life is to be a life knowing only this world and that her childhood resembles her own in no way. William has consoled her in the past by reminding Sybille it is always an impossibility for a child's life to completely resemble their parents, had not she herself done everything she could so that her own life had diverged from Hilda's? He had joked it was the reason she spoke to a strange Irish man at an art opening in the first place, or why she had gotten on that train to Berlin. Her life has always been an effort to create something new, once something became familiar. But this reasoning doesn't really work for her and so she laments the life Luzie experiences.

One morning, watching Luzie pull the zip, she thinks how morose William is being. As her daughter slips out into a new day in a new part of the country transformed by the morning light Sybille reaches out and puts a hand on him.

He breathes deeply, once, twice, thrice.

— You're allowed to be sad, you know?

— Sad?

— We've all lost someone. We don't have to pretend not to be upset.

— I'm just angry.

— Well you have reason enough.

— Angry about my dead mother and father. My lost brother who I abandoned. I'm allowed to be angry about my dead colleagues and friends and the wasted earth that's radioactive and fully out-of-bounds on the edge of the continent?

He says this with a lightness and even laughs.

— Yes, it's ok, she says with warmth.

He nods and smiles at her and gets up and out of the tent, to follow Luzie.

Sybille turns to look at Hilda who she knows is awake but who is keeping her eyes closed and then she hears William speak with good humour in his voice:

— Good morning my dear, what are you doing?

— I'm trying to wake up the bees, comes Luzie's voice. Sybille imagines her whooshing a branch over the tall grass. They are camped along the edge of what had been a carpark of some sort of logistics centre, huge ware-houses sitting dormant with articulated trucks plugged into their side like a toy play set. The evening before they didn't notice the peeling facades, the structures shedding panelling as if moulting the better to outdo their neighbour one loading bay down.

— And why are you waking up the bees?

— Because they have to wake up. They have work to do.

— What work is that? He laughs.

— To feed the plants so there's more plants.

— Yes you're right. We need more plants, don't we? We need more bees. Bees are our friends.

— Except when they bite.

— When they sting, they don't bite my dear. But yes, when they sting: that's not nice. And that's why you should be careful, you and your stick.

Sybille can see through the open tent entrance William bend down and tickle the child on her sides and how she hunches her shoulders and squeals with delight, throwing her stick away in a moment hoping as she is for more and he grabs her then and lofts her into the air, saying:

— Now who's a bee? A busy bumble bee, and he swings her down low and then up and spinning around he steps in the black ash of the fire and the child screams with happy and delighted terror. Sybille smiles and for a moment thinks of something other than sadness and hunger.

It's another hot day when they run out of food. They awake hungry and make the girl drink water even though she at first refuses and then they feed her the last of their rations, some dried meat and some berries and they watch her masticate and hush her protests.

— Something needs to happen William. Hilda is panicked because there seem to be no solutions in the day ahead.

— According to the map there's a railroad and a river not far. We should aim for there and rest this afternoon while I look for salvage and food.

An hour later they hit the railroad and from its elevation they can see the course of a river to their south and countryside rolling down to it. On the opposite bank of the river lies thick forest, a green belt uninterrupted for kilometres in either direction and beyond that a mountain range of washed grey-green with stunted wind turbines. By noon, they come to a level crossing where the road that runs away to the south is little more than a lane. William reckons out loud that it must end in a farm or homestead of some description, though the tree growth is too thick to see beyond.

— Let's head down this laneway. They didn't build level crossings for nothing.

— And if there is nothing?

— For fuck's sake Sybille! We don't have anything. Finding nothing is better than walking to nothing.

They are all beyond patience with one another and Luzie is beyond fright or rancour. A constant, dull irritation lies between them and an abject misery sits gnawing in their stomachs.

— Let's just go, Hilda says and takes Luzie by the

hand and leads them off the train track, and if there's people there we're all going to beg, no hiding. They can't refuse a child.

— They could rape and eat the child and kill us, he mutters to Sybille.

They go down the lane quietly and the sun finds its way through weakly so that the path ahead of them is cool and damp. The grass is knee length and the growth from the hedgerow is so low they have to hunker and almost crawl in places. This is a good sign, William says, this would be cut back first thing by anybody who settled between the railroad and the river. In places they have to stop and trash with the axe and trample with their feet and they are so famished and hungry they don't stop to think they may be fighting to get to nothing at all save their own demise. It is a very slow two kilometres but finally they come out into a clearing and there before them is a farmstead: they are looking at the gable of a barn and next to it the backside of a low outhouse with a gambrel roof, between the two a gateway. They pass through it not too cautiously and come into a courtyard half covered in shade that has a cobblestone floor and a rusting car squat in its middle, long grass and moss fanning out from where the shade reaches from the two storey house that stands opposite. The group stand and stare at this arrangement and study the windows for signs of life but everything hangs silent and grime-stained.

They enter slowly and cautiously, Hilda and Luzie remaining outside. They quickly find an old pantry room off the kitchen, tinned kidney beans, tomatoes, tuna.

— We need to check the entire place first, William says to Sybille. She nods silent agreement. You wait down here.

Upstairs he moves through the dusty, cobwebbed covered rooms of a 20th century farmstead. He discovers the body of the last occupant, a man judging by the clothes strewn around the otherwise orderly master bedroom. His wasted body is wrapped tight against the tremors of influenza.

He goes back downstairs, saying simply:

— There's a body. I'll deal with it later.

— Fresh?

— Dead since years. Bones. The place is ours.

They return to the others and all four of them walk to the south up over the knoll and see where the river sits square at the foot of it and they're all smiling. The view looks so pleasant, the river's waters so placid. They sit a while at its apex and study the river and its banks in either direction and nothing moves.

Back at the house they get out the map and all stand over it in the kitchen, the backdoor open and the world slowly stirring around their good fortune.

— There really isn't a town anywhere nearby, I reckon this is the railway we have just walked along.

— And that road there is the one with the level crossing.

— Then we're here somewhere. Along this bend in the river.

— I guess this is what we've been looking for, eh? He looks up and smiles at the two women.

They spend the rest of that day resting in the courtyard and washing themselves in the river. Toward late afternoon William sets about reopening the blocked up fireplaces in the kitchen and parlour, but it will take more hours of light than he currently has so they decide on a fire in the courtyard that night instead. With the thick perimeter of trees and the rise of the long hillock and the buildings themselves the place is as sheltered and hidden as any they camped in since leaving Oslo.

It is dusk when he re-enters the farmer's bedroom and pulls the covers off of the bed and then makes a bundle of the cadaver, a jangly set of bones and dried up and dusty entrails and walks down the stairs and out the door up toward the passing and while his initial plan was to fling the lot into the river he thinks it more fitting for the man to remain on the land and so he steps off the passing, and goes up to the low stone wall that runs along it and deposits his load on the other side, saying to himself how the next day he'd bury it though he never will. Then he goes back up and brings down the soiled mattress and props it up with a broken bed post above the slow fire and they spend the evening burning it up from each corner until all that is left is a bed of springs and blackened coils.

They waste no time in the coming days resurrecting the compound's previous functions as the centre of a farm: there is no livestock left but there is a field of potatoes gone wild they can harvest and grade for seed and a sprawling overgrown vegetable garden that is bountiful. William sets about making snares in the countryside, he supposes that the river will yield the odd trout. They don't know how to cultivate grain and this bothers William. But it is late summer so they have time to figure this out. After the first jubilant days William and Sybille take inventory of the salvage and put everything on the kitchen table.

— It's not bad is it? she says. I guess we need to be thankful that he didn't live near a town.

— Yeah, he obviously bought in bulk. Do you think this pasta will be any good?

— Probably won't be as we remember it, but let's see ... Might be a bit mushy.

— What we're missing is dairy. We need a cow.

— Let me just pop out to the shop and buy us one.

— Very funny. Seriously. Luzie's already way too small for her age.

— How did vegans do it?

— How do vegans do it? You think none have survived?

— Ha ha. We both seem to be very funny today, she says in her best droll voice.

— I guess we can try to find an animal, there must be some left. Lost, bleating, looking for love. But we also need to figure out grain, next spring, we need to make grain, Sybille.

— Sure. You see William, it's possible for us to do this. We can survive here. Build something.

He wordlessly starts to return the food to the pantry.

Watch how time and space fold like a sheet of paper made from pulped trees. We cry with the approaching catastrophe. We now have whole countries, Germany, Italy, tied together tautly by the train network. The colonial cancer spreads via railroad tracks, engineers' waking dreams, as they inch across Africa, the Middle East, India and down into southeast Asia. With another ten years the dominance is economic and European, reaching out as one massive structure, a machinery of communication and commerce, circling the globe.

Another advance of years, decades, and by the year 1910 the trains of Europe have their form and circuit. Hear us declaim the numbers, and feel the terror of the distances involved: 30,000 kilometres in the land of Germany; 25,000 kilometres in the land of Russia; 21,000 kilometres in the land of France. The accountancy tells the story of a patriarchy over-reaching. From Calais to Constantinople, the continent is now criss-crossable.

Never believe in assurances or appearances. By 1914 peace has reigned largely for half a century across these lands. Remember you cannot turn a train around, it is not an automobile. Nobody ever wants war. And yet there is always that something to be lost. This growing order and progress provides a timetable for conflict and by 1914 it is the railway timetable itself, that menu of civil organisation and polite society, that now doubles as the larges-cale mobilisation plan for millions of soldiers.

We ask: What is the lintel between civilisation and barbarity?

The shawdowplay of the world at noon.

You all can always walk into war, never think otherwise. It is us, time past, present, future, who ultimately decide. The hubris of time present is lost on you, and when it's not lost, it's your greatest weakness. We see the pattern of alliances, roughly France, Great Britain and Russia on one side of the chasm, and on the other Germany and the Austrian-Hungarian Empire. Extending out are other agreements, alliances and ententes, a compli-cated system of guaranteeing camaraderie in the face of the others' apparent threats, laid over all of which are at least six long-gestating mobilisation plans. The inferno ignites with the assassination of the Archduke of Austria-Hungary Franz Ferdinand: his murder forces Austria (backed up by their ally Germany) to declare war on the Kingdom of Serbia, which in turn means that Russia will back Serbia. A domino effect, slabs of iron and murder, tottering. A series of diplomatic bluffs. Germany's William II agrees that he will indeed back the Austrians and then promptly goes off on holiday. Nobody ever wants war, but it comes all the same, even when you go on vacation.

The generals have spent decades tinkering with their plans, locking them – and everyone – into an intractable war. Every little detail is worked over: once a war is announced, every man needs his designated destination and by necessity must get there on such and such a day, at such and such an hour, he will arrive at such and such a place, all by travelling on a train, which itself is a precisely calibrated coordinate moving along its obdurate circuit.

Every country has such a plan. Germany's is perhaps the most elaborate, as they plan to attack both France and Russia, east and west in a two-punch manoeuvre that means any declaration of war against Russia means they will rush first to invade France and neutralise the possibility of having a two-front war. It is called the Schlieffen Plan. Meticulously planned lunacy.

Forty days of trans-continental train movements. The murderous trains of Europe, deployed for war. William II, recently upset because his holidays have been so badly disrupted, asks if they can't possibly change the plans. He is told diffidently: they cannot. Any alteration would take six months to prepare and execute. It is a race against time and space.

The German generals don't even really remember the initial kickstart (Austria's grievance for losing their archduke and heir apparent) but then neither do the French, nor do the English and nor the Russians. They all may think they are in charge but really it's the trains and their timetables which are running the show. What is lost: many millions of lives, a certain way of life and innocence perhaps, many royal dynasties, an empire and eight million horses too.

At the end of summer, a hot one, 11,000 or so train-machines begin to shunt and judder across the breadth of Europe.

CHAPTER VI

Hilda is in a Monday morning meeting with her entire practice – Knut, her co-practitioner of almost thirty years, their two nurses Simona and Jenny, and Sigurd, their receptionist – when the ability to channel electricity stops at 9:31 am. They're talking about her retirement and the fate of the practice and none of them notice that it has stopped or the total silence that goes up around them, the entire city growing still as rupture and confusion breaks out and the world changes fundamentally. And then, when they do realise that nothing is working, including their phones, they calmly decide to close the practice and all go home, concluding that it is a blackout of some sort, nothing more.

On her walk home along Drammensveien her mind is drawn to the practice and the long history of patients and acquaintances that have grown up around it over the years and how with the passing of time she has seen some of them get better and move out of her orbit, while others are perennial patients of entire lifetimes, gifted with feet that will never not cause them pain and discomfort. Everything will break down eventually, she knows that: she looks across the street at the other people walking with her in the direction away from the city centre and thinks how her own health is no longer something she can take for granted. The fact that she is soon to stop helping people and be occupied with their health makes her wonder if she will in turn be left with just her own ageing body, a body she feels a little bit more with each passing day.

This first day of darkening, Morten arrives home some hours after her and immediately she can see that he seems more worried and panicked than she has ever seen him and this startles her. As a civil servant, he knows that this is not just a black out, but he also knows that nobody has any idea what it could be. His colleagues, including many who work directly with the government, are all shuttered into isolation and, without any idea of how to communicate, most have been told to go home and report back the next day at the normal time.

She has to calm him down but he keeps repeating:

— But Hilda, how am I supposed to know what time it is? There is no time. Fuck: there is no way to know what time it is!

Their phones don't work, nor their laptops.

There is no internet.

The day after the lights went out, she goes with Morten downtown and opens the practice and sits there, checking patients' files and open cases. Nobody comes, neither staff nor patients. On the third day, Sigurd comes, there are a lot of burned and dying people in his building and he wants to offer them what medicine and bandages they have. He is relieved to hear that the government is still active and that the country seems to be enacting some kind of plan, even if Hilda has no real details. They try to joke that they will be all laughing about these bizarre dark days in a few days' time, but when they hug goodbye it feels more momentous, like a hug brought about by a justified fear than anything else.

After closing the practice on day three, she goes to the hospital to see if she can volunteer or be of any help: she also realises she just wants to be in a centre of action and not just be at home, waiting for Morten to return with his growing hysteria and fear. There are plenty of cases at the hospital: there have been attacks and accidents and rapes, borne from the dark and disorder of the new world and the aspects of humans the darkness seems to have drawn out like a malevolent influencer of a species so ready and willing to be corrupted. She is assigned to assist in accident and emergency, much as if she was a fresh faced junior doctor days out of college. Her role is more to offer solace and soothe the terrified in-patients, as it is obvious that nobody in the hospital knows what is going on or how they can operate without electricity. The entire place hums with a barely constrained panic; as dialysis and other life supporting machines stopped working from one moment to the next, without any warning, some of the very first deaths caused by the darkening happened there. And ever since, the deaths have just mounted.

— What are you guys here for, how are you doing? she asks a handsome Pakistani couple who are holding each other gingerly.

— We were attacked and beaten, the woman says, with a voice full of anger and indignation that Hilda is surprised to welcome and encourage.

— Oh no, how terrible.

— We were at home in bed, can you imagine?

— I probably have a broken arm, the man mumbles and looks up at Hilda, surprise in his eyes and face that he should find himself at all in this situation.

— They came in and attacked us right there in our beds. Like frenzied animals. Then they started to take everything, everything from the kitchen and the television and Sid's Playstation. Everything.

— They took electrical goods?

— Yes they also took food. They weren't junkies, we've actually been broken into before – we live on the ground floor – these were kids who seemed to be just high on the darkness.

— I would imagine they robbed others.

— When the lights come back on, these motherfuckers need to be caught. Taking advantage of a situation like this, why would people do such a thing?

Hilda has nothing to say to that.

— Just hold your arm still, don't move it, she says.

Without x-ray or the ability to make a cast even, I imagine that a splint bandage will be an option.

The couple just nod and look a little confused and angry, as if none of this makes any sense: they are in hospital, this is where answers are given so that questions are solved. But this seems to her how she spends her time in the hospital: either creating more questions than existed already or trying to solve some herself. Soon the confusion dissipates and is replaced by the hysteria, the pervasive fear, the lamentation. On the second day volunteering she is greeted with a concussed teenager who crashed into another cyclist at Bislett. The other cyclist apparently died from brain injuries. Nobody was able to get a stretcher to his crumpled body in the dark of night, a team of random people who collected at the scene tried and failed to help the man until such time someone among them, their hands slick with blood, said he was dead.

Despite such horrors, these first days for Hilda are filled with a surprising, low thrill: to be part of such a collective drama makes it possible for her to feel paradoxically more connected to the world. But this will change. As Morten spends more and more time in the city at work, exposed to more rumour and hearsay, his confusion turns to a humming hysteria she knows is neither healthy nor sustainable. In those first days, they parley when he returns and she waits for him to share any new information he may have. Increasingly though it's her that is reassuring him, grounding him in questions related to what the government is actually doing.

He rails about how the fools of the Progress Party are asserting themselves in the face of the crisis and how the civil service must create their own organisational committee with the emergency services. Elected politicians don't have the means to enact actions that will mitigate the circumstances: in any case it is next to impossible to communicate any new law or vote passed in parliament to areas beyond the city. A plan goes into place to close the borders and erect checkpoints throughout the country's administrative districts: communication is sent by bicycle couriers to the main cities in the country but with no idea of what their reception will be and whether or not they will be accepted as official bearers of government orders.

— They're just bike couriers Hilda, Morten shouts in exasperation, Rasmus from transport rounded up a group of friends who work for the courier company the government use to send express documents across the city. It's like the Romans. The country is so big, it seems so futile. It will take some of them a week or more to get to the further cities.

— Yes, but there you go: think of the Romans. Think what they managed to do without electricity.

It is not only Morten either. Quite a number of people, it turns out, simply cannot remain calm in a world suddenly wrested from the clutch of ubiquitous electricity. So many questions abound that cannot be posed to the internet, that endless source of knowledge. And if this was not bad enough, telephones don't work, nor radios nor televisions. People are overcoming inherent shyness and timidity to fret and gossip with perfect strangers. Some go totally crazy and spend those first days shouting on street corners their wild, diabolical visions and ideas as to why this is happening, in turn feeding into the wheel of hearsay and far-fetched fantasy. There has been a nuclear attack; the USA has tried out some weapon called an electromagnetic pulse bomb and it has disabled Europe and the Middle East of all electricity; the Russians have turned off the gas pipelines and have hacked the networks as a prelude of attack; eastern European states are already under foreign occupation; terrorists have got their hands on dirty bombs and have pulled off the most audacious act imaginable...

These more unfounded theories are slowly debunked and dismissed and people slowly start to try and adapt to this wholly novel situation. But Hilda sees no improvement in her husband's anxiety. He's flailing in his thoughts and seemingly a lot older, as if he has stepped one day to the next into old age.

It is some weeks into the darkening when he returns with news from the rest of the world. A communication reached the government from Sweden stating that the cause is unknown but probably natural. Illness is the biggest risk from their point of view and already there is mention of the danger of influenza and the limited numbers of vaccines and antibiotics extent in their arsenal. There is a report of a major nuclear accident in the United Kingdom at Hinkley Point and the inability to confirm or deny this, indeed no communication is known to have come from the United Kingdom. (In two days time one of the bike couriers will return with some: he will return with news from Bergen where a ship docked that reported huge explosions and mass panic on the British mainland).

Both Hilda and Morten's parents are dead since many years but they both have siblings, nephews and nieces. None of whom live in Oslo. None of whom they know anything about and have no way of contacting.

— It's funny I always thought this time of my life would be fun, she says to him.

— Fun? You mean the time after you stopped working, if the lights were still on?

— Yes, retirement. Carefree, simple. Weirdly I have this tremendous sense of calm. There's nothing for us to do other than to try and survive as long as possible, care for each other and for other people. Wait for this to be fixed.

— You really think it will be fixed? I don't.

Silence in the half-light of the gloaming.

— Do you think you'll see Per and the kids?

She is asking about his brother.

— I would like to, I would like to see everyone again. Sybille.

They find it hard to talk about Sybille because they don't know what to talk about: she was in Berlin, that much they know. The only information they have in government circles is that Germany, like everywhere else, is without electricity, people are leaving cities and moving and there is civil unrest and outbreaks of disease.

But these reports are routine and have the air of being made up, written to rote.

— I have no doubt she is looking after herself. Wherever she is.

Hilda sighs and moves to get the candles ready.

— It's a shame isn't it, that she's with William? Morten says this in the same tone of voice he does all his worrying in: his hysterical tone of voice Hilda inwardly calls it.

— Let's not go there Morten. Like I said she'll look after herself. She knows about the human body. She's a medical student. And he's an … engineer.

She takes out the tray with their empty plates to the kitchen. Some days before she decided that to dwell on Sybille's existence, as they sit in the darkness of the apartment the girl grew up in, would serve the world little purpose. It would only make her incredibly sad, and Hilda is too much of a stoic to be sad.

After three months Morten's mental state starts to affect his physical health and his nervous system begins to play tricks on his mind and then his body. He develops what Hilda is pretty certain is an ulcer of some description. One morning in the wispy light of a reluctant dawn she finds him in the toilet vomiting blood and she almost cries out before regaining self-control and starts to soothe the man. She can tell just from his eyes that he is in danger of worrying himself sick further, to a point that could become critical. So she gets a towel and dampens it in the kitchen from the bottled water and presses it to his head and keeps telling him he is fine, that it looks worse than it is and if anything worry is the cause and that he needs to just stop worrying.

— Let's get you back into bed. I'm going to make a tea that will calm the lining of your stomach. I diagnose an ulcer. You know what that means?

— That I'm dying?

She laughs out loud.

— It means I'm going to go and get something for the lining of your stomach, your acids and your gut. And you need to calm down and stay calm. This is probably a stress ulcer and if it perforates we're in big trouble.

He is quiet, accepting this diagnosis and climbing into bed, an obedient patient. Immediately, Hilda prepares to leave for Ullelands Hospital to see what medicine she can obtain and tries not to wonder if she will get any at all. On the way, she curses him and his worry and stress: getting sick is the one thing they do not need in this electricless world. Everything is beginning to get more and more difficult: the toilet is out of use (and now has his stomach bile and blood along with a day or two of piss and shit) and food is beginning to run out, medicines are finite. Taps have intermittent water. Their stock of candles is slowly dwindling. Beyond their gloomy apartment, there is widespread looting with all trade having stopped pretty much as soon as the lights went out. No food or produce come from the countryside or from abroad. No boats dock and no trains or trucks approach the city full of the commonplace goods they had grown so used to being able to casually acquire on the way home from work. A bouquet of fresh flowers, cut just a dozen hours before in Holland, a block of Fourme d'Ambert cheese from France, pasteurised milk from a cow who dreamed of endless fields of grass in the hills of Ondahl, toilet paper made from recycled paper pulp in a mill in Sweden after the paper came from a Ragn-Seles depot in Lørenskog Norway.

Walking back toward the hospital once again, only this time looking for her own answers and some Omeprazol or anything similar, Hilda feels extremely tired and fatigued because she knows that there are no great answers in store for her: both she and her husband are old – 67 and 66 respectively – and their time of being strong and resilient in the face of this situation is short. If power and electricity do not come back, soon their lives will be marked for death. Morten's life, she thinks, is probably already marked for a death not far into the future, and just as this thought forms she looks up the street to see who else is on the street with her, she wants to think about something, anything else. She tells herself once more how she is safe because in the eyes of those who carry danger she is an old woman and she draws her scarf and coat around her to accentuate the appearance of one battling against the elements, fighting life's onward march.

Shouts sound from the buildings around her, people seem to be communicating from building to building that way, and then on the street up ahead there is a figure who also seems involved in this conversation. It's about food – food they found on their looting spree. She hurries past the man, who is dressed only in a shirt and whose beard is full and hair slicked back, tattoos on one arm. The kind of young man she associates with cafés in Grünerløkka and music nights in bars downtown, a hipster is the word.

— How's it going, Grandma? How about you? Have you got any loot for us?

She ignores him, hurrying past, making a show of pulling her clothes tighter around her as her blood pulses through her body and she realises that no one at this stage, at this point in history, is the same person they were some months before. The only order still in place is the restriction of people's movements, the city and beyond the city the land has all been carved up into anarchic districts that want little movement in or out because of the fear of disease and any new burden on resources. The most evil among them will win out, she tells herself, eventually the areas of division will grow so small that any community will all but be gone and each person encountered will be an island of control wrested back from all and everyone.

The hospital is pitiful. And chaotic. People turn up with their various ailments but there are almost no nurses or doctors to answer their entreaties. People are dying from the flu in their thousands. Those patients that stuck around, either because they are too incapacitated or too scared to retreat to some quiet place to die alone, are going hungry as there is no food supply to speak of: this collection of buildings has become a meeting point for the dying and not much else. A memorial to the time – not so long in the past – when there existed an immense science to the prolongation and nurturing of life. She moves through it and her will breaks, she can barely manage to not start crying or leave immediately.

Morning light is filling the building, opening up wards of beds with figures collapsed on them, or loved ones hurriedly arriving with some looted food, a bottle of water. Throughout an incessant cacophony of moaning, wailing and crying. Hilda goes quickly to the back of the main building where she knows the medicine has been stored since the day after the darkening in order to keep stock. Back then the hospital authorities were optimistic and were planning for the outage to last, at the very most, 48 hours.

She doesn't know why she is surprised to find almost nothing there, just room after room of trash and empty medicine boxes and vials, overturned drawers and shelves, the smashed remains of computer termini. Everywhere the smell of urine and faeces.

The day a knock comes to the door is the first they haven't eaten anything at all. Just tea, made from various plants she harvested in Vigelands Park, telling herself they contain nutrients, that the tea will give Morten something. He is prone in their bed and she knows that soon he will acquire bedsores. Talking comes only with great difficulty and she finds all she can do is press the hot compress on his forehead and read him poetry, the work of Bjørnson or Kjell Askildsen as well as some of his own poems. She's no longer sure he's even listening, or able to listen.

She stopped opening the door long ago but now she is resigned to death and they have nothing to lose, there is nothing for anybody to loot in any case. The loneliness of the knowledge of death is getting to her since Morten stopped talking and spends most of his time asleep. At that moment when the knock comes, the idea of opening her door feels like a good one if only because it was action that promised human contact.

— And who is this?

— Mama!

— Oh my god.

That the shock of Sybille and William's appearance doesn't kill her tells her that she isn't ready to die, not yet, and the fact of her granddaughter's existence means that there is hope in the future and the world is not ineluctably locked into a death dive of entropy and dissolution.

The confusion and effusion of emotion is great and, as the two women focus on the gurgling babe blinking in Sybille's arms, William stares somewhat alarmed at the frailty and skinniness of Hilda. He sniffs the air.

— I know, Hilda says defensively, almost apologising, all's not so well here.

They all pause for a brief moment to smell the pungent aroma, at once sour and merciless.

— This is Luzie, mama, your granddaughter.

Both women start to laugh between tears and William fishes the babe out from between them as they hug and embrace each other.

— Oh my god. How did you make it here? Where are you coming from?

— How is father? Is he alive?

— Yes! Come in, just come in now. He's not doing well but my god he will be happy to see you.

They enter the musty air of the apartment and while it isn't appalling or shocking Hilda knows that it certainly isn't the same apartment Sybille remembers, it's as if it has been stripped bear of every last excess piece of wood or item other than Morten's art collection, which eccentric and garish as that is, now gives the place a merry dash of colour that is otherwise wholly absent.

— You walked all the way from Berlin? I don't understand. Tell me everything. How old is the child?

— Let's see father. William, give me Luzie, she needs to see her grandfather.

Sybille puts down her backpack and reaches for the child and William smiles and passes over the ball of his daughter and puts his own backpack down, they are crowded in the hallway by the kitchen door and Sybille wastes no time and goes ahead through to the back of the apartment where her parents have their bedroom.

Hilda notices that William looks relieved that she and Morten are here, she tries to imagine what they must have gone through to get there. She is moved to hug him. When she does so, she realises how small and bony she has become.

— William, I am so, so happy to see you.

He doesn't say anything for a moment, just smiles, which makes her wonder if he doesn't quite believe her.

— Trust me, I think we're all happy.

The longest conversation ever had between Hilda and William:

— You're a scientist William, what do you think is the likely outcome for humanity?

— I'm an engineer, that doesn't strictly make me a scientist.

— And I'm a podiatrist but that also makes me a doctor of sorts. I would say you're invested in science.

— Then if you're a doctor what do you think will come out of this for humanity? How many of us are going to die? Will we be able to teach –

— Many are dead already, and many more will continue to die.

— I think we have to relearn again how to be human – sounds a bit grand but even if the electricity comes back tomorrow, so much has been lost. The damage done to everything from nuclear power plants and waste to satellites means that progress got reset.

— Can we have science without electricity?

— Sure, but it would be more of the theoretical kind. More Da Vinci than Oppenheimer. I don't know how you would build a bridge longer than twenty metres without electricity. Perhaps with hundreds or thousands of men. I'm more interested in our ability to learn, as in to teach, what we know or what was known. Science is an accumulation of knowledge, applied to the world around us. How do we communicate what is known without electrical means?

— You have a daughter to teach –

— But I don't know the world she lives in, the world

she is going to grow up in. Even if the lights come back on tomorrow, the world will not be the same after this. Besides, I don't know how to teach her without the tools that I had. The tools through which I learned the world.

— I always found you a somewhat odd man William, I won't lie. But I respect your way of thinking: you're logical.

— I'll take that as a compliment.

— And you somehow helped to get my daughter and granddaughter back here, so I'll always be grateful to you.

— It was the right thing to do: there's not much left other than family.

— And what about your family?

— I have no idea. We looked for my brother in Berlin, but there was no trace of him. He had gone, like so many others. That was, eh, hard … As for my parents, well, you know the same I know about Britain and the nuclear fallout. It's probably raining on us here too, who knows. And what's more, Ireland is twice removed from the mainland. I don't think it's somewhere that is possible to get to, even if I tried.

— I'm sorry.

— Thank you. It's okay. One made these life decisions, you know, when there were still planes and the internet. Decisions, as in whether to leave home and move abroad, somehow you didn't think of them. It was just, your life. The village was everywhere: Facetime allowed more family time than some enjoyed when living in the same house. I don't know. The darkening has made the world so much smaller, but in a blind way.

— Whereas before we could see each other.

— And us? What do you think we should do? It's so cold here, there's no food being grown. There's no food full stop. And I don't see where any will come from.

— I feel like I shouldn't really offer an opinion.

— Of course you should.

— I'm trying to tell you that I believe in your knowledge, and I believe in my daughter. I don't know about the world or the future of humans in this world but I do believe in you and my daughter. And granddaughter. It's a conversation to have soon.

(The conversation will continue, on and off, stilted, interrupted and often disjointed, for the years it takes Luzie to grow from a baby to a toddler to a child, back and forth, fed with the rumour and hearsay available on the street, and the ever-growing difficulty in finding food and staying warm.)

He dies around a month after their return.

His last hours are a wretched series of convulsions and expulsions from his disintegrating body, his pain is almost too much for Hilda to watch and she spends most of the time in the kitchen quietly crying, asking William whenever he enters if she is evil for wishing to kill him. He says not at all, such an action is about the only humane one left to them but he knows that he will never be able to carry out an act of euthanasia. It is abject: death has never been so private and contained and in contiguity with the living. Life now is death and to his daughter he is a dying thing, much like to him she is a living thing that needs constant protection from death.

Some hours after he has died, Sybille and William wrap the body in the very sheets it lay in. What words spoken between them are instructions that they need to wrap the bundle tighter, and then tighter still, as this stops it from moving and unravelling as they move out of the apartment and down the stairs. They bring it out into the yard that is largely earth and there by the back wall William sets about digging a shallow grave with a bowl and pan from their apartment. This takes him well into the night and it is almost totally dark by the time he pads down the earth to make the grave-mound. He has never felt so old or of the earth, he has never felt himself more mammalian, a mortal animal, and his whole body is trembling from the exertion and exercise, the nervous tremulousness of hard physical graft expended on what he sees now as an all too human act but one to which he has never given much thought. Sybille joins him then, looking on wordlessly, leaving before he has time to stand and look himself at the outcome of all his work.

The next day, she plants a small sapling, an oak from the garden on the other side of the road. William is about to tell her that it is too close to the wall, that it might not get enough sunshine but thinks better of it and says instead:

— That is nicer than any gravestone or anything.

We're crying because of all the loss, the losses ongoing, and the losses to be.

Cenotaphs are erected across the ravaged land for millions of men who never grow old like they should.

That we descant and yet again descant upon this murderous theme of the trains of Europe. After the world war and hecatomb, the German royalty abdicate – vacate – and this blasted collection of railroads becomes one organisation free of any royal assignation. It's called simply the Deutsche Reichsbahn.

The world momentarily bloats, and then crashes. In the year 1924 Germany signs the Dawes Plan for reparations; it allows for foreign investment in German industry, leading to the trains becoming a company-operated organisation that is owned by the State. It reforms itself, it becomes sophisticated at accounting, innovates with faster trains and buys the Schenker company to fight off the burgeoning competition of automobile logistics. Resentful racists and anti-semites proliferate. The train network, no matter its talk of being beyond the ken of politics, is slowly infiltrated by Nazis.

The dark, tentacled reach of the network begins slowly to groan with horror. By the year 1934, Adolf Hitler is Chancellor and the board of the Deutsche Reichsbahn Gesellschaft is overhauled. The lead railroader is called Julius Dorpmüller. Heavyset and in his sixties, he is described as a one-dimensional man whose only passion in life is the orderly running of railroads. He offers up the system to the Nazis and their diabolical project. He maintains his own, and that of the organisation he leads, distinction from politics and Nazism but in reality he, and the many thousands who work on them, facilitate and are complicit in the regime's aims. By 1938 the train network is already a site for humiliation and discrimination for Jews. It will only get worse.

Soon the story of the trains of Europe is a tale of war once more. War and genocide. War may catch the train organisation off guard but this doesn't stop them from giving the army everything it needs: 15,000 trains are deployed in the invasion of Poland in August of the year 1939. Within three weeks that country falls and its train network is subsumed into the network, becoming an organisation called the Ostbahn. Other networks will be soon plugged into the growing tentacled leviathan, those of Scandinavia, France, the Low Countries. Left to run

themselves, they are given Wehrmachtverkehrsdirektion,
armed forces transportation divisions, allowing them to
be controlled for the greater goals of the thousand years to
come of the Nazi Reich.

The rolling carriages of the dark.
Entangled histories spluttering with velocity.

CHAPTER V

He had found the notebook during her last trimester, when she stopped going far from the house. He went further and further afield through the grey, red brick city that was slowly being abandoned, looking for food and supplies for the birth. The place meant nothing to either of them, a rest station on their way elsewhere. He never felt more homeless and told himself that Sybille and the child had to become his home. He found it on the fourth floor of an office building downtown and when he realised the large, heavyset notebook – blue with a hardback cover and a couple hundred pages – was empty he knew he could gift it to Sybille. She had been talking since their very first, early Berlin days about writing a book, a plan which seemed to have returned front and centre after they had met John and the Serbian artist.

With a certain degree of hesitation he gave it to her that evening, suggesting it could be a good receptacle for writing. It was durable.

Sybille was touched by the gift: yes she felt writing could be an antidote to the world without recorded image and sound and the slow shrinking of the horizons hemming in all around them.

— Thank you. I think you found the heaviest possible notebook. They both smiled at one another. But yes, I will write. Takk.

Sybille is lying in a bed in Oslo that she slept in before, in her other life, before the darkening. There is a lot that a life can contain, she thinks: youth, middle age, old age and the ages in between those that nobody tells you about. When a life can no longer contain any more, perhaps that is when madness sets in, or some other affliction, one from the long list of afflictions we've created for ourselves: the desire to self harm, violence towards others, addiction, cynicism, a bad sense of humour. Resignation.

She thinks with nostalgia about a world that could easily afford resignation. She rubs sleep from her eyes and asks herself: how resigned are you to any of this? The darkness, the difficulties newly acquired about every waking moment? Motherhood? Is there a choice in how this day will turn out? The ritual of each day, each one a new, alien everyday she still finds hard to recognise.

Was there ever a choice?

Beside her, baby Luzie hiccups in her sleep and Sybille holds her breath a moment as she waits to see if she'll wake. They are alone in the room. In the years pre-darkening, when she first slept in the same room, she was mostly alone. Occasionally with men or Camilla. Towards the end before they left for Berlin, with William. Now, she lies staring at the window, then moves her gaze to the corner of the ceiling to its right and she tries to think back to her life before, when it was busy and not always easy but not as difficult as it is now.

She and William are back in Oslo, they made it this far after months of debate and arguments and uncertainties, of walking and camping along a road that threatened them at every moment, all the while keeping their child safe.

They kept the baby girl alive.

Her waters broke just as it was getting dark. It was two days before the spring equinox. Just over nine months since they had sex in their apartment on Reuterstrasse.

— William! William, are you there?!

— Yes, sure, I'm right here.

— My waters just broke. It's happening.

They had talked through everything they could think of and had planned the best they could: the room arranged just as she wished it to be: a mound of bedding in one half and a low stool they found in an abandoned café in the middle. Over the previous days, he had also brought as much water as he could manage into the apartment, and there it lay waiting to be boiled in their kitchen by way of the improvised fireplace which he made from an electrical stove that took a week to dismantle so that in its cavity he could keep a fire going and boil water on a tray lattice across the top, with most of the smoke being channelled into a makeshift chimney he feeds to the window. The room either unbearably hot and smoky or freezing with their breath showing, but over the weeks he had managed to keep the fire going incessantly so that the cold had been kept at bay. Everything had been sterilised. They had one bottle of bleach, some tubs of hand sanitiser she found in a bank, and lots of sheets and towels, all as clean as they could approximate clean.

And still they felt dreadfully, apocalyptically, ill prepared.

— Sybille, just keep breathing, I'm going to go and let Dea and Trygve know.

— Jesus fuck, you can't leave me now!

— This is the plan, we planned it this way.

— I don't give a fuck. You're staying here.

He had no argument and so he slicked back her hair and tried to count with her the inhalations and exhalations.

— Breath in … breath out.

The child awakens and cries out immediately upon regaining the world and her little limbs buck up and kick the air. Sybille turns and props herself up and puts a finger under Luzie's chin and the baby calms a moment and seems to concentrate on opening her eyes. Before she cries again, Sybille gets out of bed and puts on the clothes she has worn every day for the past week: a dirty, fading pair of black Levis jeans, a button-down shirt and a too-big, navy Ralph Lauren jumper. She has learned to appreciate clothes that won't fall apart too quickly: she handles items of salvage and pulls on seams and examines stitching. How they look no longer matters. This outfit comprises the only clothes she has and she is savouring the prospect of going through her own closets and seeing what clothes of hers and her subletter's remain. But she wants to be clean before putting on the new clothes.

Luzie is placid and gurgling to herself, a finger in her mouth and her legs peddling the air and Sybille goes out into the corridor, looks in the living room, ends in the kitchen. William isn't anywhere in the flat. On the table, there's a note:

I've gone out to look for food etc. Back in an hour.

It is untimed and she frowns at this and thinks once more how time has become such a slippery construction which they are only getting worse at not deploying. Back in an hour. It is about as defined as the beginning or an end of a dream. She turns around and has to stop herself from opening the fridge. Everything is so familiar and yet horribly truncated and showing signs of entropy, it is giving her vertigo. What is this kitchen in the morning without the ritual of brewing and imbibing coffee? She has changed. The world has changed. And this apartment, by its continued existence, is the same in one sense but in another wholly metaphysical context, it too has changed. She had subletted it, with the vague notion that she would return to it after a year or so in Berlin. But yes, it has changed: it has no lights, no cold fridge full of food, no TV, no kettle, no friends calling around. In her bed is her child and not a one-night stand. The place smells of damp and around the fridge is a foetid pool of stagnant water and spreading above it up the walls is an explosion of black mould. Opening the window, she stands a moment listening and all is quiet like the sound of the city first thing on an erstwhile Sunday morning, a restful abdication of any and all activity.

Just as she takes a photograph from the fridge door of herself and Camilla, their faces sneering laughter at a party in Milan, the magnet affixing it to the door an Eiffel Tower from Paris, Luzie starts to cry within and she moves, starting to coo, approaching the little ball of flesh and white linen and scoops her up into her arms, hushing the child as she does so.

She furrows her brows and makes her face into one large, consoling question mark and rocks the babe gently in her arms as she walks over to the window, just managing to move a curtain with her just-free left hand. Waldemar Thranes Gate is deserted. Full of trash and cars that lie haphazardly along it, abandoned where they had cut out. She puts the still crying child back down on the bed and takes off her jumper and undoes her shirt and removes the sports bra, which she notices is smelling pretty bad, and then lifts Luzie to her breast and walks to the armchair in the corner of the room and sits down.

The two lamps were still lit when the sun broke the dark and the room was filled with a blue light and her groaning was defining the layout of the walls, the dimensions of space itself. The candles had spluttered out long ago and William felt guilty for letting his mind wander and think with avarice that they could have been used at another time because they weren't needed during the night.

She was like some kind of wild, enraged animal with an impatience that gave her an impatient fury.

— Fuck, fuck, fuck, please just fucking fuck ... She shouted and wailed and William was beyond self-consciousness enough to ignore her abuse as he encouraged her on further and further and essayed, and failed until she was desperate enough to listen and follow his orders, to make her breathing regular and to time her pushes incrementally.

A little later and she hears steps coming up the stairs and then the door of the apartment opens and she hears that it's William.

— Good morning. Hey. We're in here.

She hears her own voice and is surprised to hear it sounding happy.

— Hi you two, he says, kicking off his shoes and putting down his backpack and the jerrycan before coming over to them.

— Did you find anything?

— As a matter of fact I did. Or rather I found information about finding things. Apparently there is a centre for people with babies where we should register. It's downtown at Youngstorget.

— Okay, well let's clean ourselves first and change clothes. We need to find you some.

— How are you? How is Luzie?

— We're good, and she laughs. She feels suddenly euphoric, as if a year of being totally pent up with worry and fear has now finally been overtaken and aired out with relief. We're good, aren't we Luzie?

He bends down and kisses her forehead before moving and opening the curtains, looking down at the empty street.

— How does it feel to be back? You seemed to sleep better.

— Well we have been camping out in nature for the last five nights so it's no surprise I slept better. But yeah: good. It feels really … good. She looks at him nervously and sees his mind working and his silence suggests he doesn't share her enthusiasm.

— I'm glad, he says and breaks away from looking at the desolate street, smiling suddenly. It's amazing we got here. That they let us in. Or me at least. He goes to the living room. Speaking of which, he continues, shouting now so she can still hear. I don't think we should lose any time. There are checkpoints right across the city. Do you think you guys will be ready to get going soon?

She can hear him sorting through their two backpacks. She has yet to go through all her things in the apartment.

— Yes, we'll be ready in a bit.

She walks back and forth, still half naked, for a number of minutes: bedroom to living room to kitchen to bathroom to bedroom until William asks, looking at her:

— Are you looking for something?

— No, she says laconically, I think I'm just saying goodbye. Again.

In the bathroom she can just about see herself in the mirror – the room has no window and so relies on the light coming from the kitchen – and she cups one of her breasts up and admires how full and firm it is. Not everything has gone to ruin, not yet. She feels dirty though, her underwear is soiled. She is sure – she knows – that she smells of baby sick and sleep, of shit and a week's worth of sweat and grime.

— I really need a wash, she says, still staring at her cupped breast, half to herself, half to William.

— Yes that's the plan. Be clean for your parents.

Sybille passed out from the pain but when she came back around she knew somewhere that this was the beginning of the end. She saw in her mind a bend of bay and fishing boats and sun, some memory from a distant holiday, and she felt the rage and the smashing of boats in a storm. Plastic bottles tossed violently in a river's weir. Cataracts of her body's fluids and she was aware that Dea was present. Time had passed. Such pain surely was the very opposite of life?

The child's head appeared by the end of the morning and soon after the full body caked in its vernix caseosa and Dea handled it while laughing and William reached for the scissors, forgetting to sterilise his hand as he had promised Sybille he would throughout and he cut the placenta then, looking anxiously at the body of the crying child and crying himself. Sybille started to sob-laugh and raised her exhausted body up enough to see her baby and say:

— I did it, I fucking did it! Oh my god she's beautiful.

— How do you know she's a girl? William couldn't help but laugh, even though his mind was genuinely curious, as if he is observing some preternatural thought process of a new mother at work.

— Because it is a girl, and she is beautiful.

All of them were crying and Dea told William to get a towel to clean off some of the vernix and then they passed her over to Sybille who had only the energy to smile, humming a kind low laughter of relief and joy.

They leave the apartment shortly after, taking the long way to the Aker river because they want to go down to

Markveien, which they find is trashed and full of detritus and lined with vacant houses, some burned out shells, a mass of telephone poles almost making it impossible to pass at one point. At the bottom of the grass bank that runs down to the river that makes up the little park called Kuba, there had been a footbridge but they see in the morning light that it has been destroyed. All that is left to indicate it once was there is a jumble of wood and trash that acts now as a ford.

William goes in first, then Sybille. She runs shrieking to the bank and then steps awkwardly and unsure-footed into the cold melt water of the river. Sybille has brought a couple of bottles from her cornucopia of former days, the gels and shampoos which have coagulated and hardened in some but still come out bright coloured and pungent. The smell of cleanliness. Sybille spends a long time lathering herself, cleaning every crack and crevice and washes her hair and William is transfixed by her as she stands half submerged in the river, the brilliant vulnerability of flesh, the gangly awkwardness of the naked body. Eventually she climbs out and runs to him laughing and gathers herself in the towel he holds up.

It takes them a long time to cross town. Everywhere they find the same trash and burned out buildings. People are going about their business, carrying water canisters or wheeling barrows with wood and other supplies, but everyone is calm and unhurried, unlike in Sweden and Germany before that. At the checkpoint they go through, there are holding pens and army and police and an air of subdued anarchy. William sees that the pens are in fact open: the people in them are sick and just don't want to die alone. Sybille overhears the grim fact that if you get influenza, you're going to probably die. She doesn't convey this to William, but a little later there is no doubt that the rancid smell that makes them want to vomit is that of unburied bodies.

The ineluctable horror of what happens next in the tale of the trains. Cursed kismet. Let's descant on, as dispassionately as possible.

There are 330,892 Jews remaining in Germany at the outbreak of the war. With the conquest of Poland, this increases by a further two million.

Heinrich Himmler, the head of the SS and German police, orders Reinhard Heydrich, head of the Reich Security Main Office, to concentrate Jews in ghettos in the newly occupied territory. These operations are done badly and so on December 21, in the year 1939, he appoints Adolf Eichmann head of office IVB4 of the Reich Security Main Office, to better oversee things. This office's purpose is to organise the movement of people to achieve the government's

*racist plans. There follow massive numbers of people re-
located: Jews are sent east, into ghettos in Warsaw, Lodz,
Lublin and elsewhere, while ethnic Germans are brought
to the west from places such as Lithuania.*

*The vibration on the mountainside shudders with the
electrical storm meeting the lowlands.*

All about the tree here we sit and cry.

*On July 31, in the year 1941 Hitler gets Hermann
Göring to order Heydrich to solve the 'Jewish question'
once and for all.*

*The trains don't stop rolling: trainloads of Jews, as
well as other so called undesirables, continue to move
east. They go to places such as Minsk, Riga, Revel. On
November 4, in the year 1941, Reichsbahn trains disgorge
20,000 people in Minsk alone, where SS Einsatzgruppen
shoot them all. The numbers are hard to imagine. Indeed
it is hard for the SS members to physically do this action
(though do it they do). But such shootings in forests at the
edge of town are not scalable. The ghettos are getting full.
Himmler feels other methods have to be found.*

*On January 20, in the year 1942, Heydrich chairs a
conference at Wannsee. This is to put in place the roles of
the various departments and their responsibilities in the
Final Solution. The protocols of the Wannsee Conference
are horrendous in their cold banality. Technologically
driven mass-murder. It is taken for granted that the
Reichsbahn can facilitate the deportation of the Jews, and
that it will remain an internal SS operation. The protocols are sent to everyone present, ensuring everyone's
culpability.*

The year 1942 sees the majority of Holocaust murders. Himmler chose the location of the ghettos based on rail accessibility, likewise the series of death factories that are next created. The SS develop a way to use a poison gas, Zyklon B, to kill humans en masse. Where train connections are good and seclusion is offered, termini are created, black marks on the soul of humanity: Belzec, Sobibor, Treblinka, Auschwitz.

A horror net is raised up across the continent, trains start to depart stations filled with Jews, Roma, homosexuals, communists. They shunt from France, the Netherlands, Belgium, Croatia, Poland. Eichmann creates and oils this network with help from the SS, and local police and military connections. It is he and his office colleagues who work with local government offices across Europe to settle on the deportation numbers, the timetables and quotas and the use of local railway lines.

Eichmann's subordinates Rolf Günther and Franz Noval arrange the final number of people and how they will be moved exactly from their location through the network to their place of doom. They then contact office twenty-one of the Reichsbahn Traffic Section to be assigned passenger carriages, or whatever carriages are available. It is Otto Stange, a 59-year-old railroad veteran, who is in charge of these Sonderzuges or 'special trains'. He drafts schedules and six times a year they meet to review them. He spends his days on the phone, arranging these trains, which are often made up of twenty third class carriages (with one second class carriage for guards) that carry 1,000 people.

As the war starts to turn against Germany, the SS pack these carriages with up to 5,000 people. Freight or livestock carriages are also used. These Viehwagon see the condemned stand for the days it takes to reach their destination, only one bucket latrine for everyone to share. Many do not survive.

One struggles to image the horror of such journeys: the squeeze of so many men, women and children, the smell, the fear, the humiliation of defecating in front of a hundred others, the exhaustion and proximity to those who die, the destitution of being ripped from your home and left with nothing, all of this borne on clanking, shunting carriages previously used in the movement of oxen.

We continue to water the tree but we cry all day.

The sun also dies but not quite yet.

We stumble on.

CHAPTER IV

Sybille is thinking about how to tell William her big news when she hears a woman crying out, in anger or pain it is hard to tell, and a man grunting. The noise is coming from around the corner, the point in the return to the apartment when Sybille quickens her pace almost to the point of running. She always feels more exposed on her own street than other streets. Since the very first day of the darkening, the flat she shares with William has come to feel less and less like a home, and more and more like a potential trap.

She is just a few doors from there now and up to this point was excited about the salvage she has to present. The thought occurs to her that if there is more than one attacker, she might not make it. The resigned inevitability of this thought surprises her. But what a sad way it would be to go, now that she has a tote bag filled with tins of food to present to William, along with her news.

When she rounds the corner she sees a strange scene she cannot immediately decipher: a teenage girl seems to be attacking an old man with the licence plate of a car. He is cowering, on the side of the footpath, as if trying to sit on the kerb, his hands raised over his head and his body scrunched up into a ball, pleading in a rhythmic grunt.

Not what she expected.

— Hey! Sybille shouts involuntarily and is not heard.

The girl is Turkish–German. The old man too. She looks up around at all the surrounding buildings, takes a step forward. There are always so many vantage points in the city for unseen, unknown eyes to look and regard your every move.

— Hey, she shouts again and jogs a step forward. Hey, stop!

This gets the girl's attention who now stops hitting and cursing the old man, her hand with the licence plate ceasing as it is raised over her head and she looks at Sybille for a moment.

— Siktir git orospu, she shouts in Turkish, bize ne yaptığını bilmiyorsun! She shouts this first at Sybille and then, as if to acknowledge that Sybille doesn't understand her, she finishes it by directing her anger at the man and then to nobody in particular, lost as she is in her own resolute anguish. As Sybille reaches them, the girl is raising her improvised weapon once more and is about to bring it down on the man. When Sybille reaches out and tries to stop her, the girl merely steps back and spits at Sybille, rage fully enveloping her.

142

With disease now killing more people than hunger or violence, this is a powerful line of attack. Sybille can do nothing but raise her hands up to cover her face as the woman lunges at her and grabs her hair and they both topple over onto the ground. They roll and Sybille then manages to get first onto her knees while keeping the thankfully lightweight girl pinned to the ground. As she stands, the old man gets up and kicks Sybille in the side of her back and she lets the woman go and turns and pushes the man hard so that he totters and falls back where he had been crouching. Both the young woman and the old man are now shrieking at Sybille as she slowly starts to turn and run away from them. They are shrieking words of indignant fury she has no means to understand. Turning the corner, she thinks of her route and how she will fend off the hunt if the hunt comes. But as she approaches the building door she looks back and sees no sign of the woman or the old man on the street and she thinks of all the people watching, all those who must have been listening and she panics at this, the covert witnesses of her shame and wretchedness. She bursts through the door and runs up the stinking stairs.

— I don't want to, but we have to leave this city.
  — But I thought you wanted to stay.
  — It's been a month. William?
  — What?
  — Nothing is going to get better. We've made this. We either get out of it alive or we die here.

For days and now weeks everything has lain together incorrectly. There is the manic confusion bred from the disconnect of the world going dark and the emergence of disease and acute hunger. Inside Sybille there has grown a strong sense of personal injustice. And this in turn disgusts her. The practice of humility and need for self effacement, the old Norwegian Jante laws, the unutterable grief of the doctor she planned to become, Christian guilt and something she takes to be a nascent mothering instinct all make it so that she feels shame toward her selfishness.

— Where will we go?

— Back home.

— You mean the Oslo plan?

— Yeah.

— But can we make it?

— We don't know that we wouldn't make it.

— Nothing moves. Nothing works. We would have to walk. There are hundreds of thousands of people – millions – with the same idea. All hungry. All infected and sick. Desperate. With no rule of law.

— Then let's walk. You said so yourself: we need to imagine the world how it was for humans through most of history. Well, they walked.

— But Sybille we don't know what's out there, who is out there and how desperate they are. This is like a horror movie or something, it's –

— Oh shut up, William. I'm supposed to be the hysterical one, the intransient one. A horror movie? What the fuck.

He frowns at this and she thinks how difficult it is to communicate, to really communicate in rational, sane ways because all anyone has to offer is confusion and fear, herself included.

— Going north. It's colder up there. And we don't know what's left. If there's any semblance of normality.

They both pause and listen as they both hear people moving up the stairwell. She thinks of the bolt on their door and breaks the silence:

— *Semblance of normality?* Are you fucking losing your mind? William, look around you, we have left the normal behind long ago, we left it on the first day. We're in the middle of a neighbourhood we have no right to be in. With only superficial reasons for arriving here in the first place. In a world I barely fucking recall. Without family. Without the language. Without the *languages*. There are people all around us who speak Turkish and Arabic as first languages, let alone German. People have no interest in us to the point that they will kill us because I would kill us if I was them –

— Sybille, please, don't say that.

— Don't say what? You're the one who is saying we don't know what lies out there. I'm saying what lies out there lies downstairs, or across the street, or around the corner. People are people. Infectious disease is infectious from … *other people* and it kills indiscriminately even if humans might try and be even more prejudiced than they already are. We need to start speaking a lot of truth because our German is shit and we are here with a European Union passport and the wonder of the Schengen Agreement –

how do I say these words in German? Or in Turkish? Or in Arabic? We came here thanks to cheap rents and because the parties were fun, because it was somewhere we could hang out with people that looked like us and who all had that magic thing humans once called money we could magically get out of the machine called a geldautomat. Oh, there's a German word you know, I wonder how much that is going to help us? We are in this city because of we like the fucking caffè lattes and contemporary visual art. Where is the art now, William? She is shouting hysterically and starting to cry. Where the fuck is the art and the life that went with it, that it was supposed to enhance?

— I didn't come for the art.

— Don't! Okay, just don't.

She is standing by the window, her arms drawing her points in the air while he stands motionless, his shoulders sloping toward the earth and old foundations that slink low below out of sight.

— And what about David?

She sighs and uncrosses her arms and wishes she wasn't an only child for the first time in many years but wills herself to show empathy.

— It's been a month, William. I'm sorry. I don't know what to say.

— Maybe you're right.

She holds her breath when he says this, stares at him obliquely, waiting.

— We're somewhere that doesn't make sense. In what the world has become. And David doesn't seem to be in the city any longer.

Her eyes express a generous sadness and she smiles when he finally looks at her. She feels a protective flicker of anger in every direction, a twist of injustice, an indignation that makes her throat suddenly contract, which makes it hard for her to swallow. Sybille draws a breath then and brings her hands together in front of her chest.

— Then let's go, he says finally, exhaling loudly. Let's get the fuck out of this city.

— I just keep thinking of all the death. How we cannot communicate with the people around us.

— I mean, David is probably dead, but we don't know that for sure. And yet I can't stop thinking about people underwater or at sea, when the lights went out. On boats or on rigs. Like what about the people on the International Space Station. Or in mines. Or –

— William! Please! I know it's hard to give up hope, but … She shakes her head, unable to find the right words to express what she wants to say.

— Okay, okay. Let's leave the city then. You're right. There's no food. Water is scarce or will become all but impossible to get once they cut it off at the reservoirs, which are mostly electrical I imagine. That will lead to no more water coming into the city. It is flat here: low water table.

— See: you're smart. We can use your fucking weird mind to survive this shit. Fi faen, she laughs trying to approximate lightheartedness, how did I end up here at the end of the world with William 'The Engineer' Day?

They leave two hours later, just after nightfall. William's logic is that in the dark, it is easier to move through the city without being seen and easier to hide should they need to. Although he worries that the sound of their movement alone in an otherwise silent plane could mean their coordinate is easy to track and locate, Sybille dimisses this concern. She feels simply that if they don't act quickly on the conversation they might never do so. She can't imagine getting a day older in this place that she has always been connected to by the most tenuous of threads. They have no reason to be here, is her re-alisation. Possibly they never had. So she starts to or-ganise their belongings straight away. They have one backpack each, which she lines with plastic bin bags. She starts to sweat.

— William? she shouts through to him in the kitchen where for his part he has started itemising the knives they own, the pots, plates, the many items they can't take, their precious six lighters and three boxes of matches, the store of candles. William, let's try and do this methodically, yeah? Come here and tell me what I'm doing wrong.

— Let's only take two changes of clothes. There's so many other things to carry. And socks, lots of socks.

— I want to see what you pack. What you pack is as much mine as yours after all. And vice versa.

— Yes. And let's leave space, we need to have space for food or anything we come across.

— Good point. And god knows we need to come across something.

— So it's around one thousand kilometres as a car drives to Oslo, but we don't have a car. Obviously. If we go at a leisurely pace of thirty kilometres a day, we could be there within a month. But I imagine that we will have to go overland and the bridges, up Jutland, Odense direction. I've no exact idea how long that will be, let's say three hundred kilometres, add on another one hundred for contingencies and we're looking at around forty-five days of walking.

She is nodding to herself as she stands over the contents of their backpacks laid out in front of her across the entire available floor of their bedroom.

— We can do that, easy, she says to him as he leaves the room and she swallows and decides now is the time to tell him before hesitating and changing her mind, involuntarily shaking her head. She looks around the room, walks out into the living room, trying to see what can be the one item she can find that would be a bridge back into the past. A book: the one piece of technology no longer totally redundant. She goes back into the bedroom and moves to the bedside table, a confusion of books and other detritus of their life that is already past tense: around the tottering book tower is an empty box of condoms, accusing, an old u-bahn ticket, an envelope with a list of numbers on it which were once a projected list of income, a tin of Nivea cream all but used up, a glass long forgotten, which had become an ornament holding a dried up rose.

From the books she fishes out from near the middle the book John gifted them, and she manages to avoid making the pile topple over. *To Warmann.* She was reading it every day during the week immediately before the darkening and has been rereading it ever since, finding solace and meaning within because she can tell herself she knows some of the characters. Suddenly she remembers John's dream and the night he told them about this, his recurring dream of mushroom clouds and apocalypse. And at the same time she recalls his laughter, self deprecating and wholesome, the sound from a time outside this time that she is currently standing in, a time that was yet unmarked and growing bright. She wonders whatever happened to John and his Serbian friends, all the people in this book, now that the world has become the nightmare and there is not much left to laugh at. The story she and William settled on was that John and David were out the night before the darkening, still in the club and that they were together when the lights went out. There had been no trace of John or David in the following days. William left tape on his brother's apartment door, sat in his kitchen for hours that sometimes turned into days, waiting for them to show up. He blames John (which by default means he blames himself) for the disappearance of his brother. Sometimes Sybille feels that the greater scale of the catastrophe is lost on him, filtered as it is through the fact that he has lost his brother as well as his old university friend as a result of it.

She will take this book: her bridge to the lost land of the electric world.

As she walks around in circles, packing and repacking their gear, she thinks how it took her a couple of days before the realisation suddenly struck her, just as she vomited up everything her stomach contained: morning sickness. At first she was worried it was the flu: they had heard at a gathering at their friends Samantha and Purcell's flat that a bad strand of flu was present in the city and that it was killing people, young, old, fit or un-fit. Electricity provided antibiotics, ICUs, paracetamol, cleaning products and functioning hospitals. Now all that is gone. This was during the first weeks of daily, unceasing panic and questioning and the creation of contingency plans and the deciphering of rumour. The search for the missing. What a time to have a child, she tells herself, but also how wonderful. She had an abor-tion before and did not tell William anything. And now: she will be a mother, no matter that everything else is in the process of falling apart, she'll create by bringing things together, usher life itself into the future.

Closing the door, she adjusts the straps on her backpack and considers once again the weight and how it feels. She can always get rid of some items if it proves too heavy. She wants to make a joke to mark that they are finally leaving but William has already started moving down the stairs, in that hesitant and expectant way one does in the pitch darkness.

— Okay, she whispers in the dark, let's go.

They take their time moving down through the building, listening all the time for any noise. Behind some of the doors they hear movement, talking. On the second floor they hear crying and the sharp, shrill shout of a woman. On the street they immediately turn right and move down Reuterstrasse, both of them hooking their thumbs underneath the straps of their backpacks and nervously straining to see or hear any movement or sound on the street. This is the first time they have been outside at night and they take in how the odd apartment lets itself be known with a soft glowing light. They have talked often about what it is people are using: William goes with candles and oil lamps, Sybille believes people are tending to open fires. Most apartments however are totally dark.

William wants to try and get a road atlas so they are going to go via Hermannplatz and look in the Hugendubel bookstore in the Karstadt department store. Sybille argues that road atlases would have been looted long ago, what with so many people moving out of the city but William says it is better to check and see. She is reluctantly agreeing when she notices the group of people right in the middle of the square, huddled around a fire. Sybille can make out two men and a woman but not much else and she doesn't know why she is surprised to see that all three of them are smoking, the orange points growing in the dark and their bodies loose in conversation as they sit on the low monument by the fireside. William and Sybille cling to the wall of the east side of the platz, hoping they are imperceptible and never once taking their eyes off the group. Sybille finds herself pleased by this group's presence, how they almost normalise in a small way the rest of the unseen city and show that not every human has become a harried animal, scared to step outdoors or commune with other humans, that some can sit around in the wide open and talk and smoke. They seem to Sybille carefree and she takes this as a good sign, a sign of hope. William whispers:

— This is dangerous. Get ready to run if need be.

The furthest they have been since the darkening is Samantha and Purcell's on Anzengruberstrasse. It hits her that they are walking into a perfect state of ignorance shaped until now only by hearsay.

Standing just inside the doorway of Karstadt, Sybille keeps a kind of look out, although the only thing she can see is the fire burning in the middle of the platz. William runs over to the book section, clumsily and too loudly in the dark, once there he flicks on the lighter in his hand and tries to find an atlas. Sybille curses as he first trips over a book stand, then crashes into a whole shelf, toppling it to the floor. The noise of his search echoes up through the multi-floor edifice in an unbearable way and she thinks again of her own private trip to the bowels of Karstadt and the secret she discovered there in the pharmacy, and weighs up again when the best time will be to tell William. She feels that if they leave the city behind safely and cover the distances in the time William has predicted, they will be in Oslo by the end of her first trimester. Hiding it will only lead to confusion and she admits to herself that she is confused as to why she is hiding it from William: she has never relied on anyone as much as she now relies on him and it is his child after all and yet there has always been something about William, from the very first moment that they met, that makes him somehow beyond the primal acts of human interaction. Her thinking is that there isn't much more of a human thing to hear than that you've made someone pregnant and that soon you'll be responsible for an innocent life that needs protection and care. The truth is she is reticent because she doesn't know how he will react and this scares her in a way she never knew she could be scared.

She is staring out into the dark of the platz when suddenly the space flickers into dancing shadows behind her and she turns to see William's figure extended below a thin flame: he has set a twist of paper alight in his effort to locate what he is looking for only it has clearly burned more rapidly than he estimated because now he is cursing and recoiling as it burns down to his hand. He drops it and it catches fire to the carpet just as it is burning itself out. He swears and starts to stamp it out and for a few seconds Sybille has an image of the whole of Karstadt on fire behind them as they run down Kottbusser Damm, fleeing the city that has been their home like some pyro-maniacal heretics. She has in her mind the image of all the buildings that have been burned out in their immediate vicinity: the first weeks saw a new fire each night as people presumably tried to light fires and torches, improvise light back into the darkness of night, and with little experience they started fires that there was no way to control or to extinguish. William suggested they were also possibly deliberate fires. Fire and infectious disease killing more people first before hunger arrived to stake its own callous claim.

— William! she hisses in the dark. Let's get the fuck out of here.

— I don't think there's anything here for us, he says, but more to himself, in an almost whisper.

— Fuck, William, come on. She is starting to panic and turns from the entrance and enters the dark of the shop, following the aisle from memory to the entrance on the north side of the shopfloor, harrying him as she moves, bumping into detritus and strewn display stands as she rounds him. Come on, come on, let's go.

The doors are smashed and the sound of crossing the broken glass is like one from a future she never expected but still recognises and she keeps telling herself: We have only one chance at this, we have only one chance at this. Over and over until William reaches her and she says:

— We've only one chance at this.

— Yes I guess we do.

— Now which way do we go again?

— Straight down Kottbusser Damm. Oranienstrasse has two bookshops and an outdoor camping shop. Then on to Alexanderplatz.

***

They don't find any road maps or atlases in the book-shops, nor in the camping shop. But William recalls that there is an auto shop a few doors further down Oranienstrasse and within it he finds a whole shelf of ADAC-issued road atlases.

— They even have a Scandinavia atlas, he shouts out to Sybille.

— Shhh, she protests.

Further along the ink-black streets she admonishes him further:

— You don't seem to realise, we've only got one chance at this. She's whispering and he's nodding his head in the dark. We can only go one direction, forward. We have no home, and we have to be quiet as fuck.

There is a wild, feral energy to the city, and it passes into them both as they move through this electric-free version of Berlin. The dark is home to the occasional orange glow of fire and the sound of people behaving in ways that pre-darkening would have been considered lunatic or maniacal. Demented singing and murderous, self-righteous prophecy. It took all but a couple of days for society to go the way of electricity. As they walk down Heinrich Heine Strasse, Sybille thinks of all the nights out she has had in so many nightclubs and bars, of the previous summer sitting outside the Spätkauf across from Kit Kat, drinking with the gang and looking at the line of revellers queue up, taxis dropping people off, tourists wide eyed. A decadent pre-run for the rapture.

At Alexanderplatz they hear large bangs back toward the river, too round and muted to be gunfire but some explosive all the same. There are figures walking through the night but not many, and the further they walk and the colder it gets, there are less and less. These people are as scared as they are, Sybille guesses.

— What time is it, do you think?

— Two, maybe three.

— Should we stick to the bigger streets or the smaller ones?

— I don't know. Prenzlauer Allee feels like a safer bet. We can see our surroundings better.

Within half an hour they are north of Danzigerstrasse, soon the ringbahn: this is further north than either have ever been on foot. At the planetarium they hear the voices of what sounds like a large crowd. As they approach they soon see that there is a fire in the grass area before the domed structure, around which sit a dozen or so people, and that they are drunk. They haven't seen any drunkenness since the darkening. There is a guitar and singing.

— Is that a couple having sex? Sybille holds William's arm to slow him down, and they move behind a car in the middle of the street, William staring over Sybille's shoulder.

— I don't know, could be.

It is hard to make out what exactly is going on but in a way it resembles a luddite celebration of the darktimes, the energy frenetic and euphoric in the firelight. This is a drunk, raucous gathering, very different from the one or two subdued gatherings they passed along the way. Hysterical laughter and a high-pitched entreaty rise out across the streets and nearby train track.

— End-of-time orgies shouldn't be a surprise, William says, moving on. After all, it's Berlin we're still in. Come on, let's keep going.

The scene makes Sybille feel that things may have been different here in the north of the city: the people were different and their experience of the blackout has been different, their response to the situation is not the same as what she has witnessed. She has no idea if this makes it less safe and, besides, she knows it is illogical: she herself argued just hours before that they had no true connection to their part of the city, and yet just by being present there had made it more readable, more recognisable than this part of town. She reminds herself that as an itinerant these thoughts not only don't make sense, they no longer apply even if they did. Every person holds within themselves a different set of responses and they are all that mattered, so that larger, collectivised responses of a locale, a region, a country – none of these constructs matter anymore.

The street opens up more and the houses become shorter, further apart. Pretty soon they are passing by the suburb of East German tower blocks, exclaves from the city that only ever had tramlines connecting them, literal outliers. The road becomes a motorway, cars strewn along it and signs of mass movement of people too: the cars have all been looted and ransacked, their petrol syphoned off and staining the road around them and in turn making the air rich with its kaleidoscopic and ethereal smell of metal. Discarded clothes hang on the meridian, some shoes, shopping trolleys with odd items of furniture.

The moon comes out and they can see the road stretch out ahead of them and the stunted chaos and detritus of a population abandoning the useless, darkened metropolis.

— Let's try and fully clear the city by sunrise, William says.

— Okay. How are you doing? She asks, trying to sound soft and casual, and not how she really feels, which is terrified and stressed.

— Good. Tired I guess, but good. I mean, we've gotten this far.

There is a boyish cheer in his voice and Sybille finds herself smiling, because it is true after all: they have cleared the city and they still have an hour of darkness.

— It feels good to be moving actually, Sybille says. A sense of control or something.

They don't stop even though it is tempting to try and look for salvage in the cars and trucks. Their sense of smell is heightened and the reek of decaying corpses make them avoid certain cars: many of those fleeing became too sick, Sybille guesses, and chose to die in a stranger's abandoned car. There are a lot of trucks and William puts that down to the day of the week and timing of the blackout. Almost all have their doors open, hanging in the dark, their insides strewn out around them, while within lie their hidden caverns. Many stink of rot and decay.

As the sky starts to brighten to their right they see a service station up ahead.

— Let's check this place out, Sybille says. We can rest a bit.

— Sure.

They cross the meridian onto the other side of the motorway and turn onto the slip road leading to the main buildings.

— This was built by the Swedish, you know.

— What was: the service station?

— Well, no, the motorway. It was called the Friendship Highway or something like that, back when the Wall was still up. Think about it, goes straight north out of the city, to the coast. Next stop, Sweden.

Sybille, smiling to herself, wonders and not for the first time, how she ended up with such company during the end of the world.

They find nothing useful in the petrol station, presumably because everyone else passing through had the same idea. The buildings are old, and feel dated in that way they do when things were built to the dictates of another dominant ideology not their own. There's a restaurant that has a jaded communist design, the building creaking in the dawn air like a sinister ghost ship harbouring past atrocities out of sight.

— Let's not go in there, Sybille says, and keeps walking toward the end of the car park. Come on, let's take a rest up there where those trees are.

The car park is surrounded by a forest of tall, narrow spruce and pine trees. She gets there first and scrambles up the embankment of sandy soil, taking off her backpack with relief. The sun is now past the horizon and everything is visible.

— Go further, don't sit there exposed to everything,

where you can be seen from the road. William is twenty metres behind her and she looks up ahead into the forest and rises to her feet again, feeling the full weight of her backpack as she hefts it with her right arm.

The first sign that something is wrong is when a window smashes into a car window behind William, near to his right. It startles him such that he lets out a holler from far back in his throat and jumps forward, ducking as he does so. At the same moment Sybille, who has reached the summit of the embankment, turns to look back but loses her footing and slides down what is a steep, sandy slope on the other side. She registers pine cones on her backside and legs.

— William! she says, panicking, not knowing what just happened.

He runs up the embankment and turns around as best he can, cumbered as he is with his backpack, and looks back at the hotel building. He sees two figures moving at a sprint, a man and a woman, the man decelerating somewhat as his arm moves above his head, slowly turning a sling, the woman holding something in her arm.

— What the fuck, William says lowly to himself before turning, scrambling down toward Sybille. Quick, get up, there are people coming.

— What? Who? Sybille is up but has to lean back and hike the straps of her backpack on, jumping up a little to absorb its weight as it sinks onto her back. William is now ahead of her, running as fast as he can. As she follows him she panic-speaks to his back.

— William! Who is it? What's going on?

She looks over her shoulder and sees through the trees two figures at the top of the embankment. The dawn is still ink-dull and it is as if the forest is shrouded in a dark shadow. She keeps running, the sand beneath her feet making it hard to get traction. William keeps looking back to check on Sybille and soon realises that whoever these two troglodytes were, with their sling-shot and angry send-off, they are not pursuing them.

— Come on, it's fine, they're not following us. He persuades her to keep moving by taking her hand in his.

— Herregud. Who the fuck were they?

They are both out of breath and sweating, adrenaline pushing them on into the forest. The land becomes a little hilly, and they run down an incline into a little opening but don't stop. Eventually they come to a halt where the trees are thick behind them and the grey strip of the motorway isn't far to their left. They pause and turn their gaze upwards, holding in their breathing, listening. There is just the dawn chorus and the sound of their own blood pulsing in their bodies.

— Okay, let's stop here.

— Herregud, Sybille swears again in Norwegian as she drops her backpack and falls down onto her ass. What was that all about?

— I don't know, but I'm just glad we didn't get to find out.

Sybille has never seen him so nervous and unsure.

— I mean we were obviously leaving, on our way, what was the point of running us off when we were already gone?

William remains standing, looking toward the motorway then up to the sky, listening all the while. Sybille has her legs up and her arms out in front of her, picking mindlessly at pine needles in the sand. She looks up at him and says the words before she thinks them through:

— William, there's something I've been meaning to tell you.

He turns and looks at her, his face open but uncertain.

— I'm pregnant.

For a moment he says nothing, just stares at her. Then a smile spreads across his face. She'd forgotten how different he looks when he smiles, how boyish.

— Daylight, she says.

— Time to find somewhere to hide.

Listen.

How to account for the conception of life itself, the birth of the sun in the first instance, the creation of progeny?

Then let it be said, we spoke of fate proper and how the Second Law is accounted for, how you create in the middle of so much wanton destruction and murder, and build within the relentless drive of entropy.

Listen.

One year after the forsaken Wannsee Conference, the year 1942, a victim of Nazi persecution gives a series of lectures in Trinity College, Dublin. Erwin Schrödinger, winner in the year 1933 of the Nobel Prize in Physics, essays to give a physicist's take on answering that most metaphysical, biological of questions: what is life? He goes about addressing organic life through the prism of physics and chemistry. His one pressing question, first given momentum by Carnot and his quest to improve the steam engine: how to account for the fact that the second law of thermodynamics states that things should move towards states of disorder and yet organic life moves into states of complex and elegant order? And what's more, life seems to cohere and order itself over time too. He asks his audience: 'How does an organism concentrate a stream of order on itself and thus escape the decay of atomic chaos mandated by the Second Law of Thermodynamics?'

The apparent paradox is accounted for by the fact that all of life exists in a system that includes its wider environment. At this moment in the story, the sun plays a constructive role: all of life on earth enjoys a free energy source from the pour of the sun, enabling us to eat, produce energy, order ourselves and expend waste.

And so each of us, in turn, contributes to a net disorder in the universe entire. Something is always lost, remember. We are not isolated bodily systems moving independently through space, our horizon is the surface of the sun and beyond that the cold reaches of the universe itself.

Schrödinger continues to outline what physics can bring to biology. He attempts to account for evolutionary ordering over time. In a universe growing ever colder, we bring so much warmth. He posits the existence of an 'aperiodic crystal', as yet unfound in the 1940s, that allows for the passing of information from parent to child, progenitor to progeny. The molecular biologist Rosalind Franklin first detects such a thing by way of her work in x-ray crystallography. In 1953, Watson and Crick build on her work *and, inspired by the lectures of Schrödinger, propose the double helix of DNA, the base pairing of nucleic acids, as the means by which genetic information is stored and copied in living organisms. Order over time.*

Only growth remains (as well as its inevitable and correlated expenditure). Entropic waste is everywhere and the train network is in ruins. And yet emerging is the growing sense that humanity has the means to overcome any and all natural impediments. The great acceleration begins in the shadow of the mushroom cloud. Technology is moving on from trains. Radar – radio detection and ranging – is developed: the art of sending out a pulsating radio wave and using its echo to situate the distance and location of an object of interest. A further closure of space and time: the world speeds up. V rocket research brings man to the moon; penicillin ushers in the antibiotic revolution.

The transistor, a semiconductor device that switches or moves electrical signals and current, a series of gates and channels that is like a microscopic train network in itself, is first developed in the 1950s. It has a direct origin in radar research during the war years. The MOSFET, or metal-oxide-semiconductor field-effect transistor to give it its full name, will go on to be the most widely fabricated item by humanity, with over thirteen sextillion produced and utilised in almost every single electronic device. All of which will be broken, one of the destinies of our sorry story.

So listen.

All things must pass into states of disorder, that is the mandate, that is the fate of things.

CHAPTER III

Sybille leans over and turns on the light and blinks against its effect, fumbling amongst the clutter of the bedstand to find William's phone. She has just found it when she feels him stir beside her. She turns to watch him slowly reach for his boxer briefs, use them to wipe himself clean of semen, throw the boxers back down beside the bed and then return onto his back beside her. His left hand rests across his chest and his right hand is curled by his ear, eyes closed. He appears to Sybille to be solemn and momentarily out of time like a Greek or Roman statue and she can tell he is dopey and sleepy from the prolactin and oxytocin coursing through his body.

She goes into the kitchen as he snoozes and puts the kettle on and opens the fridge to see what they have: she takes out the butter, cheese, cucumber and the milk, only to realise they have no fresh bread. She throws out the leftover pasta in their bowls and stacks the bowls in the sink, running water over them. She is thinking: does love get in life's way or does life get in love's way?

She brings two cups of coffee into the bedroom.

— So what about you? What did you do yesterday while I was out partying like the bad girl that I am? What is it you say you did?

— You mean the day before yesterday.

— Oh yeah, god I really have lost a day. You know what I mean.

— I went and tried to find David. He wasn't answering his phone.

— He wasn't answering his phone.

— This is Friday.

— Not yesterday.

— It reminded me of the Gaeltacht. I had a really strong déjà vu. Sometimes this city is just so silly.

— Gael-what?

— How can a foreign city remind you of the country-side in your childhood?

— Berlin is home. I don't know anything about your childhood in the countryside. You never tell me about it.

— The Gaeltacht was, still is I guess, this thing in Ireland, you go to the west during the summer holidays to learn Gaelic.

— Did you go by train? she teases.

— As a matter of fact, we did, he says with a smile, it was kind of like a summer camp. Three weeks: classes in the morning, sports in the afternoon, dancing in the evenings.

— Dancing every night?

— Traditional Irish dancing. Not that much fun. Well, fun enough I guess. There was a lot of flirting, boys and girls away from home. We would be housed in locals' houses, spread across this epic western landscape right on the Atlantic coast, stonewalls running everywhere. We didn't speak much Irish, mind. But we learned other things.

— Like what?

— How to kiss girls, he laughs and she laughs, looking at him from where she sits up in bed with her cup in two hands, while he makes a point of remaining stretched out with both hands behind his head staring straight up at the ceiling.

— David running in fields, chasing girls to kiss.

— The two times we went I was always on the lookout for David. It's why this memory came up: going over to David's flat yesterday was just like the year in the Gaeltacht when our houses were separated by around three or so kilometres of this exposed Galway road, more like a lane really. I remember his house was way out on a headland at the end of some peatfields and my *bean on tí* – the woman of the house – told me when I got in from morning classes that she had been told to send me over to his house. I think it was called *Teach Nora* – the houses were named after the women of the house. *Teach* means house in Gaelic, he says as an aside and laughs like this information is funny.

— Sounds like metal cutting wood to me.

— I have no idea what the husbands did all summer long while they hosted a dozen kids from the city. God knows we never saw them.

— Not all men are good with children.

— Anyway, I wasn't surprised because his house-mates had told me he had been sick when I asked them where he was that morning. Yesterday, this all came back to me. The long lonely walk in this exposed lane, the ocean beyond, islands, the feeling that David was sick and there was probably little I could do for him. All this while walking up the hill to Boddinstrasse!

— The day before yesterday.

— Day before, yes.

— And? Was he sick?

— No, he wasn't at home.

— No I mean as a boy, what happened when you got to him?

— Oh, well he was in a bad way. He wanted to go home! I remember finding that funny: David of all people, homesick. Turned out he had to get his appendix removed.

— Oh that's painful.

— Yeah, he was in terrible pain. Yesterday, Friday, for some reason I told myself that once again David is sick. And that he's my responsibility.

— William, how many times have I told you?

— I know but it's hard not to look out for him. This is

what I'm saying: it goes back to childhood. Even now, in this city, where all he does is party and piss his life away, I can't help but feel it's my job to make sure he doesn't stray too far...

— Yeah, well he was out, he was with that stupid fuck John.

— In Berghain?

— They were still there last I heard. Sunday's are David's favourite.

— There's been no answer on his phone. I guess he's crashed out at home.

— Or he's still there, she said with a hint of mischief. Your coffee will get cold.

— Oh shit, thanks. He raises himself up and grabs the cup, sipping it tentatively. How long can people actually spend there?

— David has been there until noon on Monday more than once.

It had been sometime since they last sat in bed like this together drinking coffee.

— But it's still so early, he says.

— Or late, depending.

— Surely David couldn't still be out. How much drugs would you need to keep going for 24 hours like that?

— William, what did I just say? She laughs but without any humour.

— I know but, but I just love, he says sarcastically, how he texts you back and doesn't text me, or answer my calls. Me, his boring older brother.

— And so, what did you do then, Mr. Boring Brother?

— I walked to the entrance of Templehof but the sun had set and people were leaving so I turned around and walked down the hill to O Tannenbaum, half thinking I'd meet David there.

— We also went to Tannenbaum, but later.

William doesn't say anything to this but just drinks his coffee. Sybille tells herself that he is probably going over what it means to be missing people like coordinates loose on a plane with trajectories that weren't destined to cross until such time that they did.

— Can I be honest? he says cheerfully.

— Sure.

— I think I moved here just to be close to David. And because some drug dealer wanted to kill me! Isn't that ridiculous? I'm really sorry I dragged you, dragged both of us, down here.

— Oh honey, don't be, you have no reason to be sorry.

— Oslo isn't my favourite place, but neither is Berlin. And David. I think I feel like I want to. I don't know. Rescue him?

— I'm glad we came to Berlin, you know that. And you know I'm fond of David too, even if I'm hard on him sometimes. And hard on you for acting like a big brother when he no longer needs a protective big brother. What he needs is a girlfriend.

— He is hard on himself too.

— I have to let go of always needing to be in control.

Sybille doesn't say anything. After a moment she puts down her mug and gets back under the duvet and hugs William around the waist. William continues to sit up thinking, drinking his coffee in small sips, looking at his phone's screen, waiting for something to happen on it. They spend the morning in the apartment, circling each other. William is the first to get out of bed and cleans up the living room from the night before, washing the dishes and loading the washing machine with laundry. Sybille falls back asleep and the dream about Iceland and 9/11 picks up where it had cut off earlier. When she awakes again it is fully day and light seeps across the room. She stretches, raising her body by arching it fully with feet and shoulder blades, and becomes for a moment a bridge.

— William? You there? she shouts out.

— Yeah, I'm in the kitchen.

He is on his laptop, jumping from one website to another.

— Could you be a darling and bring me my laptop? I think it's in the living room.

She wants to be gratuitous in her enjoyment of William. Their time together would soon be over, so why shouldn't she enjoy these little pleasantries? He comes in with a smile on his face, her laptop in his hand.

— You've become too lazy for your own good, he says with a smile.

— I know, it's terrible isn't it?

An hour passes and they both remain at their respective stations, browsing the internet. William spends his time looking at property listings, looking first at houses to rent, then to buy – in Berlin but also in Ireland, in counties like Kerry and Clare. He spends some time looking at stock markets and checks his shares. This leads him to read the last annual report of Aker Kværner, and he gets lost in it. He scrolls through the latest political turns in the fight to open up the Lofoten seabed to oil exploration.

Sybille logs into Facebook and scrolls down her Wall, clicking a number of links that lead to *Dagbladet* and *Aftenposten* articles. There was a group chat with Kari Anne, Sandra and Hanne that she contributes to with nothing more than an emoji. :o. She then spends a long time looking at the Facebook profile of a girl who's not a Friend: her name is Yael Storr and she appears in a lot of Vismara's photographs and there is something about her that Sybille is attracted to in a mindless, Facebook kind of way. After a time she shakes her head and opens another tab. She too looks at places to rent, but instead of looking only at Berlin property she opens Skyscanner.com and looks to see the cheapest destinations from Berlin. The thought occurs to her that she can spend the last 10,000 kroner in her account on just flying somewhere south and take an extended holiday before returning to Oslo. She looks at the cities of Faro, Porto, Nice and Pula. She sends a text message to her mother asking if she and her father have any upcoming holiday plans: normally they like to go to Italy or France. Perhaps she could join them.

In the kitchen she puts the kettle on and folds her arms and leaning against the counter she looks at William.

— We need bread, she says.

— Huh? Yes. I can get some in a bit.

— Well, maybe I'll go to Kaufland and do a big shop. Not sure we have much for dinner.

— Okay. He leans back in his chair and looks out to the sky, scratching his head with both his hands, yawning.

Between him and her, a shadow falls. His computer glows, buzzes and then darkens, dead, at the same moment the kettle jumps, a spark explodes, then turns off. Both of them move their bodies in response, looking at the electronic devices then at each other. Outside, a series of strange noises rise like unsure artillery. Out of the shadow between them comes a glow, a pulsing green pixelation. Sybille turns and looks into the living room.

— What the?

— The light's off in the living room.

— The fuse must have tripped.

— I just put the kettle on. Did it blow the fuse? I don't understand.

William gets up and moves past Sybille into the hall and reaches for the fusebox. When he opens it he feels heat and a static energy in the air in front of the switches.

— That's strange, he says frowning, none have tripped. But it seems like it's burned out or something.

Sybille walks into the bedroom and raises her voice so he can hear:

— My phone is dead. What's going on, William?

— I have no clue, he says quietly, almost to himself.

She moves into the corridor and they look at each other and shrug. Sybille smiles, bemused. Moving back into the kitchen William sees through the window that smoke is rising above the Neukölln Arkaden shopping centre.

— Shit, something's on fire.

— What? Where?

They look out but don't see much else as their view is onto the large, windowless south side of the shopping centre, cutting off the source of the billowy black smoke beyond it. William turns and moves to the living room, going out onto the balcony that looks out over Reuterstrasse. He doesn't understand what he's looking at: cars are stopped in the middle of the road and there is what looks like a crash at the intersection of Karl-Marx-Strasse, a number of people lying on the street, as though they have been struck down. He counts four bodies. There is a strong smell of burning and smoke. By the time Sybille joins him it is the sound that they are registering. Out of an unusual silence comes the sound of wailing, crashing and then the pop of an explosion to the north and then the low rumble of a tremor.

— Jesus fuck, William, what is going on?

— I have no idea. Not good whatever it is.

— A blackout?

— Well it certainly seems to be some sort of blackout, yeah.

— What was that explosion though?

— Beats me, he says with an unmistakable quaver of excitement in his voice.

— Blackouts don't. I mean.

— How can I be excited? This isn't a blackout.

They continue to look down onto the street, where now a woman is running from the direction of Flughafenstrasse, carrying a toddler in her arms. The child is screaming. On other balconies, across from them and to their left and right, other people, washed with confusion, appear on balconies and they too peer down onto the street. The air is becoming thick with the mephitic taste of molten plastics, of burning. In the building across the street a window cracks and smashes, allowing black smoke to plume out.

— Harregud, William! I'm getting scared now. What the fuck is going on?

He is moving through the flat, rapidly checking every electronic device and switching all of the lightswitches off, unplugging every plug.

— There's people across the road, Sybille is saying to herself, equal parts confused and scared at what she is looking at. They're trapped, William. We need to go and help them.

She hurries into the corridor and makes to put on her shoes.

— You're not going anywhere!

— What?

— Listen to me.

— William, there are people who need help. There was an old man who was waving at me for christ's sake.

— Wait, listen. He makes her turn to face him and tries to get his thoughts together: There's some kind of electrical surge or something, I don't know exactly what it could be, but whatever is going on it's super dangerous. There could be a fire in every fusebox, there could be fires throughout our own building.

— Could it be an attack?

— It's a fault.

— Could it be.

They both stop and look at each other and listen. Sybille leans forward and opens the apartment door and straight away they can both smell smoke. Acrid, hot. Adrenaline starts to course through her, like she is being chased by a ferocious animal in a field from which she doesn't know how to escape.

— What are we going to do William? she shouts.

— Hang on, William says and jumps to the kitchen where he grabs the three teatowels that are hanging off a chair then rushes into the bathroom and starts to soak them, as well as their two bathtowels.

— William there's a fire somewhere in the building. Her voice is ringed with panic and fear.

— Just a sec.

He thinks for a moment and puts the plug in the bath and turns on the taps and then he runs into the kitchen and does the same. Sybille goes into the bathroom and registers what is going on. She takes one of the towels and wraps it around her shoulders and as she makes to leave their neighbour's apartment door opens and the sleepy, confused face of Pedro, one of the many Portuguese who rotates living there, looks at her with a furrowed brow. He is in his boxershorts still and a t-shirt.

— Hey, he says sleepily, what's going on?

— There's a fire somewhere in the building! Downstairs! There's no electricity!

— Shit, he says, and retreats back into his apartment shouting in Portuguese.

Running down the stairs, Sybille shouts over her shoulder to William.

— I've gone ahead.

At each door she bangs loudly, shouting, listening for just a moment before moving on. We have the balcony, we have the balcony, she repeats to herself. She hears wailing. Impossible to know exactly where it is coming from. Everything is speeding up. Two floors below is the fire and its thick grey smoke appears to be emanating from the same place as the wailing. She puts the towel over her mouth and enters the open door, sees that the smoke's source is the fusebox and it is not on fire but is melting: a steady, goopy drip that is creating a dark, smoking puddle on the floor. She moves along the corridor, shouting, muffled through the wet towel, her eyes stinging. A woman comes out of one of the rooms, dragging behind her a body. Sybille rushes to help. She recognises this woman, who is tall and blonde and the same age as her and who is now screaming, hysterical. Sybille is surprised by how heavy the half-dressed man is and in the stairwell they drop him. It is clear he is dead but the woman starts to pump his chest. Moments later, she puts her hands to his face and moves it from side to side, crying into it. Sybille can't make out what she is saying. The German of the woman's long, prayer-like sentences is beyond her comprehension.

Sybille continues, knocking on door after door of the second and first floors. Besides that of an old Turkish couple on the first floor, who are shuffling onto the corridor when Sybille passes, all doors remain closed.

William is at her side by the time she is running out into the street. Straight away she notices how the city sounds fundamentally different, the background pitch keyed lower with a discordant layer over it made up of shouting, smashing glass, the low grumble of fire eating its way through its immediate environs. She feels disoriented in a way she never has before, the strange feeling like she's living through a disaster movie, everything blandly obvious yet deeply foreign, even repellent, to her.

People are coming out from neighbouring buildings, stunned and frantic and looking up and down the street waiting for fire engines or police cars, any cars. It is clear cars have been affected too: they are seized up in the street where they were moving and now are left frozen, paused and muted. Further down the street, at the intersection of Karl Marx Strasse, one is on fire.

The Turkish couple from the first floor come out, followed by Pedro, all of them speaking in a confused mix of German and English. They are followed by Pedro's two flatmates, who are both in their boxershorts and slippers. Some more people Sybille doesn't know come out then. William half carries the woman whose boyfriend is dead and who is now so distraught she can barely walk. He is not the only casualty: along the street other people are also carrying bodies outside, perhaps – she doesn't know – in the hope that they can be still saved. The sound of crying and panic is everywhere. Everyone has their mobile phones in their hands but it is clear that not one is working.

— We have no candles, William says to her, or any torches.

— What are you talking about?

— We have no candles. For when it gets dark.

— Are you serious? William. I mean, she waves a hand around her at the scene surrounding them.

Shock has settled over him and she sees that his mind is reacting in a way that shouldn't come as a surprise: practical and obtuse at the same time. He looks up and down the street and sighs, a long, slow sigh that seems at odds with what is happening all around them. Everyone seems to be talking at once in languages that are understandable only to those who speak them. Sybille feels like she is going to throw up so she sits down on the street instead and hangs her head between her knees and concentrates on her breathing. She hears William talk to the Portuguese. They seem to agree with William's take on things: that there has been some kind of surge in the power grid and that has blown the fuses, with enough electricity to start fires and to kill those near electronic devices. Then he is kneeling beside her, whispering among the confusion:

— Sybille, are you ok?

— That guy is dead.

— We should go around to Kaufland, to the Arkaden, and see if we can get candles. There's no point just waiting here.

— Dead, William. I helped carry him.

— I know. We got lucky. Sybille? Come on. Are you ok?

— I'm okay.

— Good.

— I never touched a dead body before.

— Can you stand up?

She nods and gets to her feet and puts her arm around his waist and concentrates on smelling him and focusing on their feet, not looking up at the growing groups of people waving their dead mobile phones and shouting at each other in a cacophony that seems to her then like an answer to why people invented stories like Babel or hell itself. On everyone's face is writ fear, the disability to communicate with one another constitutes real terror.

Sybille notices William hesitate and turn, like he was going to tell the Portuguese where they are going before thinking the better of it, and she follows him as he turns to walk away, up the street. The three Portuguese are consoling the woman whose boyfriend is dead. It looks like she is ignoring them.

— I don't know what's going on, but we have to stick together, ok?

– Sure, she says. Where do you think I'd go exactly?

They turn left, past the Sandman bar and toward the hulking edifice of the shopping centre. People are running past them and ahead of them, some sort of scuffle or argument is taking place on Flughafenstrasse. They start to jog, a slow trot, as if to keep pace with events, fuelled by the adrenaline, fear and panic that is palpable in the air.

— Let's go straight downstairs to Kaufland, Sybille says, running ahead, leading the way as she moves through the glass doors and up the steps into the main concourse. The shopping centre is echoing with shouts and hoots like a menagerie of owls and startled songbirds.

— Not many here, William says, shaking his head in confusion.

They run down the frozen escalators and see that there are some people down below at the entrance to Kaufland. There is a group of people trying to enter the store with two employees, a young man and an older woman, keeping them out with raised arms and shakes of their heads. It's clear that the would-be customers are bottle collectors who have turned up to cash in the pfand deposit on the bottles they have spent the night and day before collecting out of bins, on the streets, out of bushes.

— Können wir etwas kaufen? Sybille shouts over them in her bad German. The bottle collectors are complaining that they can't cash in their bottles because the machine is out of order and discussing in gravelly, whiny voices possible theories for what is going on. They each have big bags and some trollies full to overflowing. Down there, it is very dark: the Kaufland supermarket takes up the entire basement level of the shopping centre and Sybille wonders if perhaps the workers in the shop don't quite realise the extent of the blackout. It has only been what, a quarter of an hour? There is no smoke or smell of burning material that she can make out and she notices that at the checkout there are a number of people who are passing over cash for goods and the staff are writing down their purchases.

— That's gonna mess up their stock system, William says. I'm surprised they're allowing any shopping at all.

— Bitte! Können wir etwas kaufen? Wir brauchen nur die dinge für der toilette.

The sole staff member, harried by the bottle collectors, abandons her position at the entrance, waving them in before saying redundantly:

— Nur bargeld ja, only cash.

They are jogging again. The darkness of the aisles makes them giddy with disorientation, a strong sense of the illicit.

— It's like in the movies, she says as she walks into the wine section only to realise William isn't behind her as she thought he was. William! she shouts.

— Over here. Come here.

She retraces her steps back to the vegetable section where William is now pushing a shopping trolley.

— We need to get all the non-perishable goods we can.

— Not just candles, then?

She is smiling in the dark and a sudden and surprising sense of calm comes over her.

— Not just candles. And we're going to have to leave out the back.

— The front leads to the stairs.

— Through the loading bay. Or whatever.

— If we can find it? Her smile turns into a somewhat incredulous, giddy laugh.

— Well, do you have cash? Your wallet? We have no other choice.

— No, she says, her excitement increasing, I mean

I could go back and get it but you're right. This is all absurd.

— There'll be mobs here soon, panic buying toilet paper, looting, who knows what.

— This is all absurd.

— It is absurd, fuck. They'll close the store any minute, they don't realise what's going on outside.

Sybille can tell he is growing frantic with the logic of his own reasoning.

— Yeah, let's find the loading bay. We can run.

— We need to just take what we can now, we can always make a list. I dunno. Pay later. Okay?

— Okay. Someone shouts behind them in the direction of the escalators, something about a dog. There is laughter, someone is being good humoured about the blackout. The layout of the supermarket is unusual but will work to their advantage because it is triangulated into the corner of the shopping centre floorplan: the customer enters to the right of the checkouts and is led around a u-bend of aisles and various food sections. The staff that are present seem to be congregating at the checkouts, exchanging information and theories about what was going on and what they should do. No one is paying attention to the aisles by the entrance.

— Oh god, oh god, this is fucking crazy. Okay. But yes. Okay. Let's do it.

They push the trolley ahead of them and move through the aisles, loading the trolley carefully in order to ensure they can fill it fully.

— Let's try and stick together so we don't double up.

Tins of all kinds: stews, tuna, beans, lentils, chick-peas, chopped tomatoes. Pasta. Rice. Jars of pickled vegetables: in the dark they include things they would never normally buy, like peaches, sauerkraut. Two bottles of whiskey. Chocolate. UHT milk. Crackers. Flour. Sybille throws in a fish for the sake of it, they will eat it the same day. They keep throwing stuff into the trolley until there is no space left.

— Okay come on, let's get out of here.

— Where's the back door? Sybille hisses. She is almost close to giggling from her nervous excitement. She keeps thinking she sees bodies moving in the corner of her eye, shadows flitting in and out of the gloom. The voices are babbling still by the cash registers, beyond the tall aisles that divide up the space.

— The loading bay is over that side, we pass its entrance coming here, William says, walking ahead. Sybille starts going over what they could say or do when they come across a staff member. She's not sure if she has the courage for this. At the same time, she is surprised by how quickly her self-consciousness and embarrassment at behaving in this way has been overridden by other, more primal impulses she knew nothing about until now.

Moving along the back aisle, as far away from the checkouts as possible, their eyes adjust to the dark but still everything is shrouded in black and gloom, and the voices and laughter seem demotic now, tense. As they pass through the stockroom's electronic doors, forevermore stuck in the open position, the space opens up, the temperature cooler and the smell rougher, a mixture of garbage and new plastic freshly unsealed with an overlay of cleaning detergent.

— Which way? Sybille whispers.

 They stop a moment.

— Not sure.

— It must be this way.

— That's where the street is.

Ahead of them stand towers of food and product deliveries stacked on pallets, wrapped in cellophane plastic.

— Come on, let's check it out.

Just as they start to move into the forest of stacked pallets, a figure emerges out of the gloom and walks toward them. It is a young woman and she is making her way hesitantly in the penumbra, one arm outstretched. She moves past them without any acknowledgement, too scared to stop or to care who she is sharing the unwelcoming place that her usually bright and cheery workplace has become. She had just smoked a cigarette: the scent memory of it fills the air. As they move ahead they see another large break in the space, light, blue and grey, it defines the space and the ceiling disappears ahead of them as the loading bay reveals itself. They quicken their movement.

— Hallo?

— Fuck, exhales William.

— Halt!

The voice is directly behind them and it is that of the controller, the teacher, the supervisor, the shop assistant as you try and steal a shopping trolley of food through the back door of the supermarket.

— Fuck, William spits out while not stopping: come on, don't stop.

— Hallo? Hey! The voice was now indignant, moving closer.

— William, shit what do we do?

They push their way through the large plastic flaps that are like thick translucent cuts of vellum hanging down from above and blink in the shadowy daylight of the loading bay. A truck, its rear doors open and half unloaded, is up ahead and William runs to the edge of the concrete platform and looks either side of it.

— Hey, was ist hier los?

Their pursuer, their supervisor, is a fat, tall man with a goatee and glasses. Sybille imagines him playing computer games whenever he isn't being a dick to the people he manages in the supermarket. He's now close enough for her to read his nametag: Herr Stolz.

The man reaches and almost takes a hold of William's upper arm but he spins himself around and bats Stolz away.

— Don't fucking touch me, William shouts. Wir machen mit Rechnung, ok?

Sybille thinks, that makes no sense: why would they send an invoice to the supermarket? Then she thinks, how the fuck are we going to get this fucking shopping trolley down from this platform? Then she imagines Herr Stolz thinking that whatever is going on it is verboten, these Americans are stealing.

— Das ist nicht erlaubt! Stolz, obviously unsure what to do next, makes to take a hold of the shopping trolley

190

just as William starts to drag it to the side of the truck's open door where there is space enough to start transferring its contents to the ground below.

— Herr Stolz, bitte, wir will zurückkommen. Mit Geld. Bitte. Jetzt es gibt keine andere Möglichkeit. Sybille is trying to distract him from the trolley, touching his arm in turn.

William suddenly turns and pushes him forcibly.

— Just fuck off, he shouts, and let us get out of here, ok!

Sybille has never heard such fury in William's voice before. But neither has she seen him shaking like he is, or his shirt so saturated with sweat. When he starts to take items out of the trolley, Sybille follows his lead, they are scrabbling like harried and desperate fugitives and then the store employee starts to shake, his head moving rapidly from side to side, and he swears long and slow under his breath.

— Ach du Scheiße…

Then his whole body starts to tremble in earnest and he blinks his eyes rapidly. From across the loading bay comes the sound of teenagers shouting and laughing: a group comes into view, all of them running and shouting merrily over their shoulders and Herr Stolz frowns and as he does so a car that is being pushed by a group of men comes into view, like a slow, silent and tired-out pursuer of the teenagers.

The trolley is now half empty and William puts his foot on the front wheel and slowly tips it over, sliding the remaining items out of the basket and then jumps down from the platform onto the ground. He stands on a jar of something and it cracks and splinters and he swears as the slow breakage joins all the rest: the city is a cacophonous soundscape of glass breaking, shouts and entreaties, and the slow rumble of collapse in the void left from the electrical vacuum.

Even when things are broken and at their worst, life is conceived and plans are made. You people, inevitably, stumble onwards. It's what all your children are programmed to do. Ever onwards out of the ruins.

Europe is once again on the move, as it always and forever has been. There are over fourteen million refugees forced to move in the years after the war. This is Year Zero. Trains and their nadir, their aid in the extinguishing of six million lives, and more, the never parallel lines of dreams and hope, all snuffed out by forces beyond easy comprehension. The scale and reach of the connected hyperobject is inhumane.

Those that do survive are played with like a cat plays with a mouse petrified by fear. Train lines abruptly end in craters. There is endless waiting at junctions of rubble.

The difficulty in travel can be seen with Primo Levi. He survives the death camp, but must then arc out of the clutches of evil, and enter the network for his nostos. First he's shunted to Ukraine, then up into Belorussia before circling back through Moldova, Romania, Hungary and Austria, before finally reaching his home in Italy. Across Europe, one in three are on the move and there is nothing but swirling chaos. Many survive on less than one thousand calories a day.

The Allies have full control of the trains of Europe. The story of the German network bifurcates in two at this point: from 1949 the eastern section remains the Deutsche Reichsbahn in the communist-ruled German Democratic Republic. It shuffles on, monolithic, the country's biggest employer for a few years. Mostly it's used to leverage Russian war reparations: entire factories are dismantled and put on trains bound to Russia where they will inevitably sit to rot. In West Germany, a new company is formed, the Deutsche Bundesbahn.

Money pours in from America. Industrial growth is the goal. It will pay for the new welfare states being created, and this welfare which ensures the prosperity of the populations, will in turn spur more growth. The double play between citizen spending and government investment is compared by economists to a piston.

Everyone is terrified of the possibility that the nadir will return. Talk begins of the United States of Europe. Trains, like industry, need steel. More and more steel. Europe starts a long journey of connecting itself up into a peaceful continent. And trains are to be the starting point.

The European Coal and Steel Community comes into be-
ing on July 1 in the year 1952. Belgium, France, Italy,
Luxembourg, the Netherlands and West Germany, all al-
low for the free movement of trains across their borders.

We watch on with curiosity and the world-tree grows
without notice, its roots out of sight.

CHAPTER II

The pair stand in the carriage as the u-bahn lurches its way through the underground passage, both holding an overhead rail and letting their bodies slightly sway to the movement of the train. This time William has insisted they buy tickets. They are going to an art opening in Mitte to which they've been invited by John, William's old university friend from Dublin. Earlier in the day it was a source of strife. Anything these days seems to cause strife but not the same kind of acrimony that they have come to Berlin to escape from, the all-or-nothing strife that was the hallmark of their last days in Oslo. Their best friends in the city, Samantha and Purcell, joke that they are the oddest couple in a world of many odd couples. But this is what made their being together interesting for Sybille in the first place.

Now, as William looks at Sybille blankly, taking a drink from the Berliner Pilsner he holds in his other hand, she can tell by his expression that he is calculating something and she guffaws then with fake dismay, and turns her head away and takes out her phone and scrolls mindlessly.

Sybille is hoping a distraction will present itself from within her resolutely connected phone: that an invite elsewhere will be issued and she thinks, as the doors close (Zurück bleiben bitte!), that she still has time to find an excuse and thus avoid spending the night with William and his friend John.

They alight at Weinmeisterstrasse u-bahnhof and move down along its blue-grey space to the far end, exiting onto Rosenthaler Strasse just as a tram rattles by, ringing its bell in protest at a group of two men and a woman who dash, disoriented, in front of its path. The evening light is fading as they make their way up Gipstrasse and on the corner the streetlight blinks on just as they approach it, and Sybille nudges William, playfully.

— Did you see that? We made it turn on.

He frowns and laughs a dismissal.

— Should we stop and get something to eat? she asks outside Café Europa. Save us having to get something later.

— If you want, I think I'm ok, William says, looking in at the full café.

For a brief moment, it seems to Sybille that everyone in the entire restaurant has their back to the two of them, it's as if not one person is sitting facing the window.

— Um, I don't know, I guess we can wait.

They walk on and round the corner onto Auguststrasse, where they pass another young couple, a dog walker, some older people Sybille guesses to be tourists. The city is tremendously still and calm and appears depopulated. As though it is holding its breath.

— You've never taken me dancing.

— Haven't I?

— Remember you said you would take me dancing?

They're walking past the Clärchens Ballhaus, a nineteenth century ballroom set back from the street with a large, messy and almost overgrown biergarten in front of it – a stage in summertime for busy dining and socialising, though this evening there seems to be just one party on the patio by the entrance, a single wayward waiter who is talking animatedly to them.

— Did I? You mean in there? He laughs once more and she finds herself being glad that their mood together has grown light, tinged with playful teasing.

— We should go later. Ballroom dancing is a much more elegant way to spend an evening than at some bullshit art exhibition talking nonsense.

— I don't know about that.

— Or at some bar. After a pause she adds: We should take John to Berghain!

— I'm not sure he'd like Berghain.

— You mean you're not sure you like Berghain? Just because you always get turned away.

— Well, he's with friends, he came from Paris with friends, it's their exhibition.

— If I get bored I'm going to leave, just saying. Samantha and Purcell have a party they're going to later in Kreuzberg.

They pass under the archway into the institution's courtyard and William, awkwardly, places the beer bottle down on a bench that is almost hidden by the trees that are growing behind it. Once inside the building, they move toward the main gallery space, from where the hubbub is emanating.

The back wall is emblazoned with huge black letters in paint that drips and runs to the floor. Sybille moves away from William and stares at the message, whose words seem to have an almost nonhuman quality, even as the handwriting has a slapdash appearance that lends the text some personality.

WORLD'S END IN WRITING

The thought suddenly comes to her that she can return at any moment to Oslo: she doesn't have to be here in Berlin. In fact, if she really interrogates her life honestly and without the need to justify any part of it, is it not true that she finds it boring?

Sighing, she turns away from the text and feels immensely tired as she approaches William.

— Sybille, look who I found.

John looks older than she expected but also more put together, well kept, he smiles and leans in to give her a kiss on each of her cheeks, graceful and quick.

— How wonderful to meet you at last Sybille, the woman who managed to not run in fear at the oddity of William Day!

Immediately she does not like this man, it is obvious he has always played the cool friend and needs the likes of William to elevate himself by shitting on them. She wants to shout at William not to put up with this asshole one second longer but instead she is being introduced to another man who she only then notices: taller than the others and older, he has a head of scruffy hair and wears wireframe glasses and, most noticeably, a white suit. John is making the introduction in a mock officious way that she isn't sure she should in fact take seriously or not:

— Sybille this is Herr Milos Lubarda, the one and only.

— Hi, pleased to meet you. She shakes his hand and is disarmed by his smile, the flicker of apology she perceives there for the presence of John, for the tone of condescension that hangs in the air around their meeting. This silent knowing between everyone, along with the fact that everyone has something to hawk or flaunt, even when they don't, is why she doesn't like art openings. That and the fact that she worries she doesn't understand the art. World's end in writing? She thinks: this is simply pretentious and I don't need to worry about getting it.

— Milos was just talking about the work, William says, pointing at the back wall and the text across it. About how it's an elaborate joke.

— Not exactly a joke, but it could be, he says in a bashful manner that surprises and confuses Sybille a little.

— It's your work? she asks.

— Not exactly.

— It's an LGB Group piece officially, John interjects, but Milos came up with it. Just don't tell anyone. The work is only ever signed collectively these days.

Sybille has no idea what he is talking about and looks at William to see if he shows signs of comprehension, before reminding herself that he never shows anything much through facial expression. So she asks Milos:

— And how do you and John know each other?

— I published *To Warmann,* says John. Ever since I've been working with Milos on getting their back catalogue translated and into print.

— Okay, Sybille says simply, not wishing to betray both the reflexive dislike she is feeling towards this man and her own ignorance at what he just said. Cool. Well then, let's get a drink!

The opening passes quickly as a series of interrupted conversations and introductions to people who appear to have various ways of socialising the occasion: Sybille realises that what she is witness to is a form of rehearsal, or rather it's a rehearsed form. A girl called Patty with two braids manically hops from foot to foot and only asks Sybille questions about herself before darting off. A couple from Belgrade tell her that they are unimpressed by the art and sad for Milos, informing her that her follow-up question – what exactly makes them sad? – is naïve. She finds them slightly terrifying and is glad when they drift off to get a drink.

After that, for the most part, she and William stand by the entrance to the bar, a glass structure that abuts the building in the courtyard, a shard of mirrors that slices the space in two, with John constantly moving between them and the bar to talk with people and to order drinks. Sybille identifies this particular performance of John's as what they call networking. But she's unsure what its end is exactly.

— What is it that John actually does? she asks William. Like, what is he doing here?

— He's getting that couple a drink it seems.

— Skipping the queue it's called.

— He's a publisher. And curator?

— A publisher and curator.

— Yeah. I dunno. William shrugs.

She is happy to see Milos return from the bar: despite the fact he looks like he has slept in the same tatty white suit for the last week, he makes her smile, there is the lightness of good humour to him that makes him stand out when compared to everyone else she has met this evening.

— Tell me Milos, is John like, your manager?

This makes him laugh to the point that he doesn't answer the question: it appears her question is so silly it doesn't warrant answering.

Later, they all go to a bar in a large group made up of stragglers and friends of friends. If Sybille felt self conscious before she no longer does because she realises that nobody really cares about her or indeed anyone else: whoever needs to know anything about anyone else already does so and everyone else is just getting drunk and having themselves a weekend night, art or no art, knowledge or ignorance. The bar is called Bar Drei and it is right at the end of Linienstrasse, in the dark corner of the city where the Volksbühne theatre sits squat, dominating like a socialist bunker.

Inside the bar counter is a square of drinkers filling out the room on each side of it and with two sides of the entire place filled with windows it has a cinematic feel, like Hopper's painting viewed from the inside. It is a film set and everyone is in the frame.

Fresh Kölsch beer is served in tall, thin Kölsch glasses straight from a barrel that sits behind one of the corners of the bar counter, the music is good and not techno – John Maus, Animal Collective, Talking Heads – and inebriation has entered the group and makes everyone shout at each other in between bouts of laughter and extended trips to the toilet. As the night goes on, Sybille finds herself wanting to tell Milos everything, even as she realises she doesn't know what she wants to tell him. He is a man, she has noticed, who makes people smile as easily as he makes them pause and consider what they are saying.

— I would like to write.

— Well, then you should write.

— Something would need to happen first.

— Things happen always.

— I don't know what I could write about. I mean I write a diary sometimes.

— Have you a copy of the book John published? By Djordje?

— No.

— You should read it. John! Give me a copy of *To Warmann,* Sybille and William don't have a copy yet.

John hesitates before searching for his bag among everyone's coats by the window: it is obvious to Sybille that he doesn't wish for her to be a recipient of a copy, and she rapidly deduces that this is probably because, all things considered, Sybille is no curator or reviewer, she is of no importance – all this she figures out in the instant of his hesitation and it makes her certain she will get a copy, just to spite the conceited fuck, yet one more man who thinks he has more to say than she has, who overlooks her position in the world because of some unnamed power structure soaked in entitlement.

— Yes, I demand a copy! she laughs and knows that only William will see the falsity but he's not paying attention, drunk as he is.

John just nods.

— And me too, I also demand! Milos shouts over the din of the bar and waves his hand to hurry the exchange along and John fishes out a copy and passes it over, unable to mask his displeasure.

— And what is it about?

— It's a love letter basically. One of the most beautiful and sad stories, really. Djordje wrote it before killing himself.

— And who is he? Sybille asks, noticing John frown.

— He was my best friend, and leader of our group. He was the manifesto writer, you could say.

— I'm sorry he died.

— It's okay. You can read book, you will see. It's like

he writes extended letter to his dead lover Warmann. It begins as an attempt at explaining our art, The LGB Group's art, but really, it's a love letter.

(Both John and Milos will live out the immediate days of the darkening but to very different ends. At least they have been brought together with the rest of the cast of this story, if only for a short while. Milos will fly from Berlin back to Paris, the train being too expensive, he will complain. When the darkening comes he will decide to go south and try to walk all the way to Belgrade but will not make it, dying from pneumonia after catching influenza. He will succumb in a display bed in the IKEA store outside of Budapest, surrounded by his beloved objects of the everyday, presented in one of those everyday cathedrals that had doubled as a furniture store. John meanwhile will stay on in the city after the opening, wanting to collect money in person from a crooked art bookshop masquerading as a distributor and see some art exhibitions as well as to party, finding Berlin laid back and fun in a way Paris wasn't. He will spend his evenings drinking beer outside spätkaufs, drawing up a seemingly endless list of contrasts with Paris and forging brief, intense relationships with several other characters drifting through the Kreuzberg summer. William's brother David and he are party buddies from Dublin, they always enjoyed each other's company and so they will spend a lot of the week together. John will dedicate considerable time to scoring drugs and moving between apartments. On the Saturday night he and David will enter Berghain and lose themselves there. When the darkening comes they will find themselves in a confused, euphoric crowd in the huge chamber of the nightclub. They will follow the crowd out into the daylight of the morning streets, and driven by drugs and a collective sense of mounting excitement, move toward the river and Kater Blau, the other well-known club that has extensive riverside sections, where confusion and drug-addled chaos will greet them. They will stumble around with the hundreds of other revellers, not that interested in the blackout or its cause, scoring more drugs. To compensate for the lack of music, some people will start to swim in the river Spree, and soon hundreds of naked clubbers join them, laughing and playing, some people fucking, the scene is mesmeric for John and David until, right out in the middle of the river, David will go under and disappear out of sight, never to be found. John will die later that day in an altercation, the end of the first day, as he tries to acquire some booze and food in the ransacked Lidl on Heinrich-Heine-Strasse.)

The week after the exhibition opening Moderat are always being played in the apartment: plangent techno that speaks of loss. Sybille puts 'Rusty Nails' on repeat and finds herself getting a lump in her throat but doesn't know exactly why, as if a loss is approaching which she has yet to fully comprehend and which in turn only makes it all the more plaintive. A growing sense of abandonment, vague and amorphous but there all the same. She speaks with William less and less and spends less time inside the flat. She visits Samantha but only when she knows it will be just Sam and Holly the dog. She likes the dog the most, she has often joked, and could easily spend an hour mindlessly playing with her. While Samantha is bathing Holly on the Monday, Sybille stands by the door looking on and feels the faint intimations of wanting to be a mother, and the thought leads her to her own mother and she sees more clearly why they argued sometimes, why her mother finds it so hard to accept William and why she finds it hard to understand Sybille taking time off study, deferring a whole academic year to come to Berlin and do nothing in particular. Her mother is sensible and calm in the face of the known world whereas Sybille is always excited, or wants to be excited, by the unknown and strange. She has no answers to her mother's questions because she doesn't want to hear the questions in the first place. Being in Berlin is question enough.

During the first months in the city she found herself texting her old friend Camilla back in Oslo, but increasingly her reports from home seemed so terribly vapid they made Sybille feel trapped – as though Camilla's uninteresting life acted as an obstacle to Sybille returning to Oslo even as her escapist plans in Berlin feel somehow blocked. The result is that these Facebook Messenger chats seem to take place in an awful, claustrophobic non-place. Even now she can't imagine returning there, to the boring bars and crushing routine, the faces she always has to pretend not to recognise, the forced estrangement from other bodies in space. And yet at the same time she knows she will eventually, inevitably, one day return.

On the Tuesday she goes to The Melbourne Canteen on Pannierstrasse, ordering a cappuccino she doesn't really want, with the intention of formulating these thoughts and feelings and writing in the expensive Moleskine notebook she bought that morning in Karstadt. After sitting staring at the street and playing with the word 'lonely' in her mind, writing nothing, she switches cafés and goes to Five Elephants on Reichenberger Strasse, where she stares at the Congo river on the huge map of Africa that hangs on one of the walls. She finds herself trying to flirt with the cute barista, unsuccessfully. Faces she recognises come and go and she has two short chats about parties, recent nights out and friends in common, first with Dora an Icelandic artist and then soon after with a Greek woman whose name she can never remember. These brief conversations make her feel calm and help her to pick up her pen and write, little bursts of words about the people around her, about friends like Samantha and Purcell, Aude, the Frenchwoman from the yoga class she goes to once a week in Neukölln. But then she stops, unable to write beyond these faint, quick lines of character portraits.

She can't drink any more coffee so goes for a walk along the Landwehrkanal, wondering why it is that she feels lonely. She has a friend network, a boyfriend, and

yet the register of her world seems wholly flat and un-
appealing. Back at the apartment, she lies on the bed
and reads. William is out working or doing whatever he
does – she simply doesn't know sometimes what he is
doing with his time these days and has no inclination
to ask him. After a while, she gets up and sits on the
sofa in the living room of Reuterstrasse 14 and reads.
She started *To Warmann* the day before as a way to in-
spire her own efforts at writing, and she recalls Milos
and the strange aura of resignation and mystery around
the guy. She realises now that for all her proximity to
these people, having partied and spent the better part
of a weekend in each other's company, she has no idea
what this book is really about, what stories it contains
or who it is that is telling them. It's like a mystery, the
tunnel of ignorance you want to rush through as a read-
er the quicker to find out the truth in the bright light
of day. She reads and time slows down further still and
she furrows her brow more and more in concentration:
she reads frowning and twirling her hair somnolently,
incessantly.

She starts to read the book a second time after
she finishes it, and then a third. By Friday she is in
Samantha and Purcell's with the evangelical mission of
recommending the book she's just finished and wishes
everyone to read.

— Have you read this book *To Warmann?*
— No.
— What do you know about the wars in Yugoslavia?
— Very little I suppose, says Purcell.

— The country collapsed, hazards Samantha, nationalism flared up, the Serbs fought the Bosnians, the Croats fought the Serbs … There was a siege in Sarajevo. NATO conducted a bombing campaign. Then Kosovo?

— That was something else, Purcell adds fallaciously.

Sybille just shakes her head ever so slightly and frowns once again: this is not the conversation she intended.

Do you want to have a child?

Are you ever scared of the future?

Could you ever imagine separating?

Does art really talk backwards to the past?

Later that night, trying to fall asleep, she crosses the page and walks in on the narrator Djordje Bojic and his lover Warmann. She wants to say to them: you love each other but don't know what to do with the boredom of love. You must see that art is the result of your love, the art of being together, you say it yourselves: the art of the humdrum everyday brings you together. I want to have a baby because that is the past talking to the future, the only way I have to get out of the present. And because like you say: the world is going to end soon.

During the next week, the blank pages of Sybille's notebook accumulate and she finds herself thinking more and more of her promise to Milos: that she will write. She finds herself frowning more often than not. She doesn't like to frown: she's scared of the crow's feet it may go on to create, she feels it makes her look old. The time left to her to express something of her unanswered questioning is running out she suspects and in her mind she starts to count down the days to when she will email her department to enrol in the next academic year. Every night she visits Samantha and Purcell and drinks wine, smokes the occasional joint, moves away from the blank pages of mute expression and lazily holds forth in the loud chatter of socialising.

This particular weekend begins with Sybille rereading the last pages of *To Warmann* on the toilet. When William returns to the flat, she waits for him to take off his jacket and shoes and move into the living room before she takes some toilet paper, wipes herself and flushes. She has lost track of how long she's been sitting there reading. Starting the shower, she strips off and stares at herself in the sink's mirror as she waits for the water to get fully hot. She feels like crying. She takes a very long shower, going over her options without realising that that is what she is doing, enumerating branching narratives for the future, termini ahead that will be ephemeral, ineffable – wholly non-existent and impossible, like the ability to quantify the amount of water each droplet contributes to the puddle or the knowledge of where they originate and to where they will flow. She can drop it all: Berlin, Oslo, and go south to the light, palm trees, skies checked with wispy contrails and scented with oranges, lavender and the sea. Valencia or Faro. Only the recollection of William's consistent irritation at her lengthy ablutions, and how likely it is that he will come knocking on the door – something which she really could do without right at that moment – makes her break her trance-like state and open her eyes and blink, open her mouth and gulp and finally turn off the current. Then she runs her hands over her forehead and hair and along her body, wiping down streamlets of water. Drying herself she realises she shouldn't talk to William, not right now, not with how she is feeling and so she forgoes the underwear she was wearing and puts on the same clothes as before, telling herself she will be back later and can dress properly then. All she does is quickly apply some Nivea moisturiser, stare at herself for a moment, put her underwear and bra in the washbasket, breathe out forcibly and then slip out of the apartment as silently as a shadow.

Outside on the street she immediately feels lighter and without giving it a thought she goes into the Neukölln Arkaden, riding the escalators downstairs, taking in the bright, Saturday evening infused faces of the shoppers, everyone looking like they are somewhat bored, indifferent under the bright lights, merging into the flattened interior of just another shopping centre. In Kaufland she buys two bottles of Portuguese vinho verde and a packet of paprika flavoured crisps and texts Samantha and Purcell without needing a reply. She is outside their door five minutes later.

— Woah, it's warm in here! Sybille says as soon as she steps into the apartment. It is a mild evening and their apartment is oppressively warm, the air humid, their radiators still set to winter settings and clothes, she can smell, are obviously drying somewhere within.

— Let me open some windows, Samantha says and goes ahead down the corridor, disappearing into the bedroom, while Sybille moves into the kitchen, wasting no time in finding the bottle opener, opening one of the bottles and pouring two glasses before putting the bottle in the fridge and the unopened one in the freezer compartment, getting two ice cubes as she does and slips them into the waiting glasses. She sits down and is on her own for quite some time – at Samantha and Purcell's one isn't entertained and that is (at least for Sybille, William sometimes finds it confusing) part of the charm: it is easy to spend time there, in the past she's hung out so long that she wound up sleeping over, on the large sofa in the spacious living room. The doorbell, shrill and metallic, an actual bell, sounds and Sybille shouts:

— Don't worry, I'll get it. She opens the front door of the apartment, returns to the kitchen, wondering who it is. She tucks her feet under her and starts to paw at the tobacco and rolling papers on the table, then to scroll through Purcell's open MacBook Pro, putting on some music.

— Still listening to Moderat! Mina Vismara shouts as she takes off her shoes. Hello dear, how are you?

Mina is a friend of the apartment, an Argentinian artist who Sybille likes for her mischievous sense of purpose, how she's often to be found in O Tannenbaum at 3am sober and holding court, then next day be found in Five Elephants, busy writing on her laptop, notebooks strewn around her, talking Spanish excitedly into her headphones – all in stark contrast to what Sybille currently feels is her own mute inability to express anything much at all.

— Vismara! Sybille is surprised to hear how excited her own voice sounds, before realising she has spent the last two days in her own company. How cool that you're here, how's it going?

The two women hug and hold each other's arms a moment, then the Argentine starts to pull at her clothing, unwraps her scarf, tugs off her jacket.

— Ai, but it is hot in here.

— Take that glass there, I poured it for Samantha but she's in the shower or something.

— Oh how I need this. Salaude!

— Cheers.

Just then Samantha walks in:

— Buenos dias Vismara, Samantha says in an exaggerated accent before bursting out laughing, good humouredly making fun of herself and the world in that way Sybille likes and envies, a manner that makes it impossible not to be attracted to her.

— I need a coffee, I can't shake this siesta I had. She sets about turning on the hob and filling a moka pot with coffee and then, joining them at the table, she leans over and says, Do you mind, I've got this album stuck in my head, and she clicks through to a song by Caribou, a swirling, shrieking house song that Sybille finds a little sleazy.

— I feel like going out tonight. Who's in?

Later they leave and go to meet some of Vismara's friends at a project space in the souterrain rooms of an old, squat building on Schönstedtstrasse. Some Portuguese artists are having an exhibition opening and performance. They hang out in the darkly lit corridor drinking Sagres beer like it is exotic, eating macadamias from out of their slippery shells.

Everything is leading to a nocturnal endpoint but Sybille can't fully imagine it, she has nothing other than her desire to go out into the city, abound in the night and its potential and this is all that sustains her as she listens to the conversation around her.

— Where's William this evening? Purcell has joined them and Sybille almost jumps with surprise because she hadn't noticed her in the dark of the corner space they had bunched up into, their bags and coats piled in front of them at their feet.

— To be honest I've no idea. She finds herself resenting having to discuss William with Purcell, though it is no surprise that she asked about him before anything else. In this reaction she finds what she intimated in Oslo, what felt suddenly like a long, long time in the past but was barely nine months before: she doesn't love William and the shock of this fact makes her fake a bright smile and ask:

— And how are you? What've you been up to? You weren't at home earlier.

It is hard to listen to her response: the truth being that the two women circle each other with barely suppressed apathy, if not outright dislike. Sure, Sybille can see that it comes down to Purcell's loyalty to William, based perhaps on the fact of their both being Irish or whatever or that they studied together, or that Sybille is more articulate in expressing the problems in their relationship and that leads Purcell to defend William out of some sense of fairness, but mostly Sybille suspects it stems from her own close relationship with Samantha. That Purcell's sympathy for William stems from jealousy. In that very moment, Sybille is aware of her proximity to Samantha, the electricity that it generates in her. As Purcell talks about her job babysitting in Mitte, Sybille imagines Samantha's posture being forced, that she is keeping her arm loose and to her side so that it was only a breath away from her own tingling hand…

— What's funny? Purcell cuts out of her monologue to ask.

— Oh, it's nothing. Sybille is laughing at the line of her thoughts and shakes her head, trying to come up with a convincing lie, this being one more easy thing about Samantha and Purcell after all, despite the distribution of friendship: they can always all laugh about inconsequential, invisible things.

— Come on then, let's get out of here.

They head up Sonnenallee, six laughing women, past the cafés and shisha joints, stopping inevitably for a drink in O Tannenbaum, a dive bar slotted into the street between a café and an electrical store, the doorfront easily missed if you didn't know it was there. Everybody in their extended circle passes through the bar, run by a group of Dutch guys, all DJs, the music always good and the beer Belgium, Dutch, Flemish, those heady, strong and tasteful beers Sybille avoids but which William loves. But she doesn't want to think about William right now.

Their group gets bigger and they pile out the door toward Hermannplatz to catch the U8 north, their friend Jules is playing at Tape Club, a monthly club night that is actually an exhibition. Everyone is shouting their opinion in the carriage full of inebriated metro riders, midnight Saturday being one of the busiest, rowdiest hours on the U8.

— It's a shit exhibition to be in, nobody cares what the show is, it's badly hung, it's badly curated.

— Curated? Baby girl, there ain't no curator to speak of.

— And then you have this large-ass art opening crowd, shifting their feet with glasses in their hand, sober as fuck. That ain't a club crowd.

— It isn't anything.

And the group laugh at this, denigrating the event they are headed to, free of any self-consciousness, a listless acceptance in their voices.

Hours later the night is moving as if on a scale, tipping in one direction before sliding back the other way. They ride the M5 tram to Rosenthaler Platz and it is like a ship at sea. Jules is making the entire tram stare and laugh and and it seems to Sybille everyone wants to be her. Sybille herself feels like she is on a hunt, the wild hunt of Odin: they are in the sky above the nighttime city, the destruction out of sight because it has yet to come. MDMA races through her blood and gives her a looseness and glow, her cheeks burning warm and the tips of her fingers enjoying everything they touch. Down Torstrasse they parade, pointlessly chit chatting with boring tourists outside Kaffee Burger. Jules and Mira are texting with a guy who keeps receding away like a mystery to a puzzle they want to solve: Louis is his name and he first said he would meet them in Neue Odessa bar, then in Kaffee Burger, now he says Wild at Heart. They get more to drink in the Spätkauf on Schonhauser Allee and sit on each others' knees, waiting and anticipating but also just being perfectly in the present tense of the night, hunting for mystery.

—I want to go to Berghain, Sybille half shouts: she has heard back from David that he and John are in the club.

—It's Saturday night, I never go on a Saturday. Sunday is where it's at.

—Isn't Ben Klock playing tomorrow?

She texts David back to say that they plan to go tomorrow lunchtime.

It is a bright morning by the time they return to Hermannplatz, as if the dark of night never happened at all. Sunlight, low and watery, pools behind eyelids that droop over pupils. Only Vismara has sunglasses and Sybille and Samantha are left to complain in jealousy that she is too glamorous for her own good. The streets are mostly deserted save a bus, some other groups of people who are still out from the night before, some old Omas on their way to who knows where. Their chatter is a little demented, inchoate, yet driven with the assertiveness of the coke they did when they finally caught up

with Louis in the toilets of 8MM bar. The cadence led by
the memory of red, blue flashing lights and their strob-
ing trace memory behind their pupils. Vismara clatters
off toward her home on Weichselstrasse and Sybille follows Samantha and Purcell without even inviting herself, it feels like there is just still something to discover,
some part of the mystery to discuss, a last drink to have.
She isn't going to go back to Reuterstrasse 14: she is
not going to return to William. She does not know if
she ever wanted to *return to William,* it seems now such
a primitive way of thinking and being in the world, a
semantics based on subdued submissiveness. Where
has she gone if she needs to return somewhere? Why,
goddammit, would anyone rely on anyone else?

— Let's have a last drink? Sybille says, wheeling
around the small space of the kitchen.

— Sure. Samantha reaches for glasses.

— I'll see you in the next life, Purcell shouts behind
her, disappearing into the back room.

Now that they are on their own Sybille searches for
the words it feels as though the entire night has been
leading toward – the utterance that will solve the equa-
tion of their inebriation.

But nothing comes to mind.

— Cheers me dear!

— Cheers!

They are drinking Campari, neat, sickly sweet and
sticky. Both are standing and as Samantha starts to say
something about the night that has just been, catching
some stray thought about a detail four hours before,

Sybille turns into her and kisses her on the mouth, forcibly, until she feels Samantha return the kiss. They both hold each other with their one free arm, tasting the mix of Campari and cigarettes, and they move a half revolution on the kitchen floor, Sybille letting out a soft moan and then they separate, Samantha smiling as Sybille's face freezes into a look of confusion.

— Sybille Helgason, looking for more than just one last drink! She laughs and downs the contents of her glass, tapping Sybille playfully on the nose. I think it's time for bed. In the morning we'll all know what the meaning of life is. Until then, we dream.

And with that she turns and leaves Sybille, who laughs to herself, wholly drunk and suddenly exhausted. She sits at the table, fishing her dead phone out more for something to do than anything else and plugs it into the cable coming from Purcell's MacBook. She thinks of when she last kissed a girl. Camilla in Oslo. An old form of communicating to William through rebellion. Only kissing someone isn't exactly a rebellion. She frowns, tries to concentrate on the view outside the window.

Her phone wakes. Blinks messages from William and one from David: he and John are still in the club, going strong.

She tells herself to go to sleep, and that all games start again.

All games start again. The words echo in her mind. She is in the foetal position, light hazes and flares behind closed eyes and she is aware of bodies moving in the space in front of her from the sound they make.

A door closes. A phone pings.

— Hey there, vagabond.

She opens her eyes and there is William leaning against the door, arms crossed, a smile on his face, the same smile that makes him appear the child he in so many ways is and she feels instantly the remorse of a future self, projected into the very near future, a few frames ahead, who has to let this man-child go and sever the connection their lives have shared up until that point. Her mouth is wholly dry and she sits up on the sofa, still clothed, the pungent smell of her hair, clothes, wafting cigarettes and alcohol and she shifts and rolls onto her back, wrinkling her nose then pinching it.

— Urgh. What time is it?

— Think it's around 3pm. Purcell just let me in. I can make coffee, you want some? The last question he asks from the kitchen.

— Can you bring me some water? She sits up, puts her feet on the ground. When he does not return, she stands and stretches and is surprised to feel her head is clear and relatively pain free, which she attributes somewhat to the drugs as she blinks her eyes fully open. Then she pads into the kitchen, looks with disgust at the Campari bottle and the two glasses on the table.

— Good night?

— Yeah. Yeah it was actually.

— What did you guys do?

— Pfff … We went out … She trails off, thinking back through the night and realises she doesn't want to share it with William, she wouldn't be able to explain what it was she had been doing, what she had been trying to find – yes that was the word: she had been looking to *find* something. We went to some bars, a club. Still frames: of Samantha, of Jules dancing on the tram, the toilet full of bodies. The shrieking of that Caribou song. She shakes her head. It was fun. A fun night. How about you, what did you get up to?

— I had dinner. Then worked a bit. Did you hear from David?

— He's at Berghain. Or at least he was. We planned to go today. But that's not going to happen.

— Is John with him?

— I presume so.

They sit in silence. As Sybille wakes up more she thinks she might start crying but crying only makes things worse – especially with William involved.

The water starts hissing and gurgling in the pot, passing up into the upper chamber infused as dark coffee, alchemical, and he brings it over to the table and she throws down three casters, watches as he gets two mugs and then stares with an intensity borne from a mind not fully awake as he pours out two cups. They sit drinking in silence and she realises that he knows the conclusion she has come to, even if she herself could not express it exactly if he asked her to. When she looks up after setting her mug down on the table, he is looking out the window at the treefingers of the linden that occupies the courtyard.

— Shall we just go?

— Let's. After we drink some coffee.

She scribbles a note for Samantha and Purcell and closes the door silently behind them and goes down the stairs, stepping with the ease that's aided by electric light.

It is the last hour of daylight and she feels a tremendous sense of homecoming when they enter Reuterstrasse 14 and she puts this down to the realisation that they have in fact made a home here and that a new fact is emerging: they will soon disband it. Or at least she is going to leave it.

— You know we need to talk?

— Yes, I guess we do.

— Maybe just not right this instant. Right now I need to get out of these clothes and wash myself.

— Sure. You stink, he jokes, trying to lighten the mood.

She finds herself back in the bathroom, listening as William walks back and forth from the bedroom to the kitchen, humming indistinctly, a trait he shares with his brother David. This time she isn't feeling as circumspect as the day before, she isn't feeling anything. She goes through the motions of her ablutions and spends time moisturising her entire body. Then, dressed in a t-shirt and pants, she sits on the couch in the living room and shouts into the kitchen:

— Are you going to cook food? Please say yes.

He returns, a bowl in one hand and a glass of orange juice in the other.

— Maybe you should start with some breakfast?

— Oh yes, thank you so much.

— How do you feel?

— Actually remarkably good, all things considered. I don't even know when we went to bed. But I'm starving. I need stodge. I need carbohydrates.

Later William sets about getting the overhead projector running while Sybille cooks, frying some chopped onions and garlic, some bacon she cuts with the plastic scissors they use for food, seasoning all of this with more salt than usual. The boiled pasta is ready soon after, she keeps some of the water back, adding the pasta to the pan and then a dollop of crème fraiche, cracking an egg, the last one in the box, and then turning it all into itself, the gas turned off, the mix cooking itself in its own trapped heat.

— It's almost done, she shouts into the living room as she passes. She dishes out two bowls of the pasta and grates the last of the parmesan on top of each. The evening turns into night beyond the window and it grows fully dark. Instead of talking, they watch *Avatar* and Sybille dozes off half way through. She awakens in the depth of the night, the room glowing orange and green from the sodium lights on the street and the power cable plugged into the side of the MacBook. The wall opposite is blue, the words *Standby* moving across the frame of the projected light. William has put the checked throw over her and she feels grateful for it, a momentary fear of leaving him rising up which she pushes back down. She gets up, sleepy and a little dazed, and shuffles into the bedroom and gets into the bed beside his sleeping, warm body.

When she wakes some hours later, her body clock is out of kilter after staying up the entire night and sleeping at Samantha and Purcell's during the day. She doesn't know what time it is, has to fish around for William's phone to see that it is 6am, dawn. The city outside is quiet and she can clearly hear William's breathing, a soft, sonorous breath that she is surprised to find herself enjoying the sound of: it is calming. For the next hour she drifts in and out of wakefulness and her thoughts move from one practical point to another that she needs to discuss with William, her emotional demands have to be made clear because she knows she can't rely on William to be generous when it comes to making the necessary effort at separating. She has vivid dreams that wash into her thoughts about her life, her immediate planning, logistics, discussing with William how they will break up. *A real break up this time.* Clichés and tantrums, friends who in the dreams turn into movie celebrities, locations shifting from Neukölln to the Norwegian countryside. Then her dream setting gets taken over by emergency, a version of 9/11. Iceland.

— You're awake, aren't you? she says, realising that his breathing has changed. She opens her eyes wide and keeps them open.

— Yes, he says simply and does not move, keeping his back to her.

— How do you feel?

— Sad … I think. A little confused. He turns onto his back and stares up at the ceiling.

— William. She puts her hand on his and doesn't say anything more. Again, she has that melancholic feeling that turns into a fear that she is being incredibly selfish.

— It's okay. I agree. Ultimately. He sighs. If you return to Oslo and I to Ireland … to Dublin I guess … then the future will be better than the past. It's logic. I just have to pick it apart. You know, like in my mind. I have to get used to it. As an idea.

She moves her hand over his onto the rise of his stomach and breathes out as if trying to summon strength, or to give his words space the better to be understood. They lie silently like this for a while and she is aware that they have already done all the hard work: they have separated and agreed to the overall terms, the details of which can be sorted out later, and with a minimum of debate, indeed a lack of conversation in general: they are now laying in bed together with no shared claim over the future. Tomorrow is a plan to face solo. Where she is expecting strife there is just this peace: unexpected and free of charge, sad certainly but not trauma-inducing, she is grateful and feels then, as the morning rises all around them, a great tenderness toward this strange man she intuits will always play a role in her life, a presence that will come and go certainly but whose opinion, whose mind, she will rely on for its ability to analyse the chaos of an emotional world.

She feels him move, he raises his body, arching it slightly and his hip moves and she moves her hand down until she feels his erection constrained in his briefs and she spreads her hand over it and feels within herself a small ache and softness and they both breathe out. Then they turn into each other and kiss and their hands move along their bodies and she pushes into him and rolls him onto his back, taking his head between her hands, she rubs herself against him and she sits back and their eyes lock and there is a swirl of everything between them and she proceeds down, pulling his briefs and freeing his cock into the air.

— I always loved your cock, she says, and she means it and she wants to give it a valedictory kiss and is overcome with a greed for it.

— Fuck, he says.

And she frees her mouth from him and she moves up, pulling her underwear aside and guiding his cock into her.

— I'll always let you fuck me, she groans and arches, oh god.

He moves his hands up under her t-shirt and traces a caress over her breasts, catching her nipples loosely, and she writhes on him, slinging her head forward, her hair fanning out into the light, his hips thrusting up off the bed in rhythm to her movements.

— How do you want to fuck me?

— From behind.

She gets off him and lays forward on her elbows, her arms out, her left hand taking a hold of the headboard, raising her ass. William moves between her legs and grabs her by the waist and she groans as he moves inside her and she moves one hand then to her clitoris and she feels out her orgasm in the not too faraway distance, it comes closer as he moves into and against her harder and when he comes she arches up into him, rubbing her orgasm into a force of sensation that spreads out through her body, down her limbs and she groans inarticulate, overcome.

— Fuck, he says, collapsing onto the bed next to her.

We tend the world-tree with water and song.

Let's start the story at the beginning, let's retreat into the past. Before the child, before the DB Tower at Potsdamer Platz. We have a couple arriving at our beginning on a train.

The end of the world is perpetually reoccurring: it happens with Watt and the discovery that the burning of carbon can power engines through the creation of steam. It happens with the detonation of the atomic bomb. It happens with an eruption on the surface of the sun.

We continue always to water the world-tree and sing this warning out into time future because that's what we're determined to do.

Technology runs into every fissure. The second law means that for all the output, all the material progress of the years after the war, there is always more of that which is lost, wasted. The greater control or domination you feel you have over nature, the entropic two step ensures that it is nature that dominates you.

Trains enjoy mixed fortunes.

The trains of Europe continue to run and are developed in some ways, but discontinued altogether in others. Planes and automobiles become ever more popular. Eventually, when people realise they are living in the end-time, they begin to favour the train, believing it is better for the environment as that mode of transport creates less waste than when trying to break free of earth's gravity.

Les Trains a Grande Vitesse are proposed in the 1960s. They run on an automated signalling system, their drivers are blind to any signal due to the speed by which the trains move. In the 1970s the Trans Europe Express connects one hundred and forty cities across half a dozen countries. By the year 1985 Deutsche Bahn develops its InterCity Express trains. And on May 1, in the year 1988 the ICE V model sets a world record of 406.9 kilometres per hour. Computer systems are installed across the network. Steps are taken to join up the European operating systems. On July 29 of the year 1991 resolution 91/440/EEC is passed, creating the European Rail Traffic Management System. In November of the year 1989 the Berlin Wall falls. West German trains start to run on eastern lines. In the Einigungsvertrag – the reunification treaty – article 26 stipulates that the two companies DR and DB will merge as soon as possible. In the year 1994 the Bahnreform turns the new Deutsche Bahn into a stock corporation with the government being the sole stakeholder. In May of that same year the continent is physically connected with trains running through a fifty kilometre long tunnel underneath the Channel or La Manche. During the years 1998 and 2000 work on Potsdamer Platz takes place in Berlin, large construction work that fills the former green- field site. This includes plans for a new office tower, which will be twenty-six stories tall and will open its doors in the year 2001. By the year 2006, Deutsche Bahn moves in and makes it their headquarters.

As Germany reunites and comes together another coun- try, Yugoslavia, starts to fall apart. And while the Hamburg to Berlin line is prioritised in the Verkehrs- projekte Deutsche Einheit – the German Unity Transport Project – another intercity line is being disconnected, de- coupled. Known as The Olympic Express in its heyday, the Belgrade to Sarajevo trainline stops running around one month after Bosnia and Herzegovina declare independ- ence on March 3 in the year 1992. War arrives once more.

The sea starts to boil and steam rises up to touch the sky.

CHAPTER I

They are sitting in the train, waiting to leave Hamburg Hauptbahnhof. Ninety-six minutes away from their destination. They have travelled through the night and have slept very little.

— I'm really glad we decided to travel by train, William says. All my favourite trips involve trains.

— I slept badly though, Sybille says.

— I remember one trip. And afterwards, David surprising me. I mean there's many things I don't understand about my brother but… Each summer we would holiday in Galway and Connemara and our parents for some reason always took us by train. I loved it. I think it's one reason why I became an engineer.

— I wonder if the restaurant is open.

— This one summer, on the night of our return I found David under his blankets crying. The poor guy was distraught. What's the matter, I asked. And he goes, I don't want to grow up. And he meant it. He didn't want us to stop going on holidays to Galway every summer.

— Oh the poor child, Sybille says, opening her eyes wide.

— Growing old is like the tracks of a train fanning out across the land, William continues, but Sybille is not really listening. And death perhaps is like a train crash. Although of course not all trains crash, he says as an afterthought, frowning.

He continues to speak to Sybille with his eyes closed, oblivious to whether she is listening or not. He's getting lost in the epic that is the machine within which they sit, itself sat atop the parallel lines of cast iron metal that reach out endlessly across the landmass.

People are entering the carriage. An old man, stooped and well dressed, struggles with his suitcase in the overhead rack. Sybille jumps up and helps him and he smiles diffidently at her and she, somewhat confused having travelled through three different language regions overnight and still sleepy, says in French, idiotically:

— Je vous en prie. She draws her mouth back into a cringing rictus before laughing out loud to the old man's bemusement and reminds herself she is in fact in Germany but this man's eye sparkle and he replies, as if trying to accommodate her linguistic confusion by answering a question:

— Merci beaucoup!

236

She turns, still smiling, and asks William:

— Eh? Strange man, stop being such a weirdo. Do you want a coffee?

He is intoning to himself an excerpt from an infinite description of his own devising that lists all he can name of the European train network, his eyes still closed and his head tilted back between headrest and window, fighting sleep with an effort at recollection and recall. He opens his eyes and smiles, interrupts his monologue and nods his head before resting his head back and continuing.

— The knuckle, coupler, axle. Jubilee, mikado, mogul. Kinematic envelope, insulated joints, signal boxes. Crankshaft, piston, cylinder …

When she returns from the restaurant carriage, William is sitting up in his seat and gazing out at the early morning commuters, tapping the glass with his index finger. There seems to be a delay: the train has yet to move. He receives the warm cup with two hands, smiles thanks and turns back to the view of Hamburg Hauptbahnhof.

— You know, he goes on, as if the conversation never stopped, the funny thing is that it shouldn't be a surprise.

Sybille tucks stray hair behind her ears and arranges herself by tucking a leg under a thigh.

— Uh-huh, she says by way of indicating she is listening.

— The train journey: making a little boy aware of his ultimate demise. The changing nature of everything, living organisms most of all. Time's forward motion and its great revenge: entropy.

Sybille sips her coffee and doesn't say anything as ever so slowly the train starts to move. Sybille has a strong sense of vection: for an extended moment she thinks they are moving as they pull away from the station, the train next to theirs gliding by and being left behind, only for her to realise it is the train she sits in which is staying still, being left behind, and the train outside the window that is moving into the future, to its destination, wherever that may be.

— How did we get here? she asks, as if trying to distract him. The two of us, you and me. So many chance occurrences.

— We got to where we are thanks to engineers, William says.

— Oh William, please, and she laughs. We met by chance, outside the opening of an art exhibition.

— Don't laugh, it's true. You got a tram that night, no? You got to Bislett by the number 8 line from downtown.

She shakes her head, smiling and says, You're the worst. Ours is a love story. Engineers have nothing to do with it.

— But we're in a train right now, he says teasingly. And trains started with steam and a guy called Watt. An engineer from Scotland. And thanks to his invention the Brits defeated Napoleon at Waterloo. This made another engineer, a guy called Carnot come along, trying to do his country some good, to help get revenge I guess, and he was like: it was the Brits' use of steam to produce the war machine, coal, steel, guns, that led them to victory. So he asked: how can France do better?

— How do you know all this? Where do you get it from?

— The British effectively invented it, a new technology. And between themselves and America they made a head start over other European countries.

— That's ironic.

— What is?

— Well look at France and Germany, they have better railway systems.

— Perhaps. Today. Not then. It was their export to the world. They started it.

— You are such a nerd, do you know that, she says laughing gaily, unsure herself if she wants to remonstrate or flatter.

— What? He says mock-indignant.

— Why do you even know so much about trains?

— I'm an engineer!

— Yeah, but you build like, pipes, under the sea.

— Yes but my first love was always trains.

William's boyish delight is clear to Sybille, the innocent infatuation of youth hasn't gone anywhere.

— And besides, pipes under the sea, extracting oil. It's just as destructive.

— I didn't know what you did was destructive, she says laughing, sipping her coffee, fully awake now and part of the conversation.

— Sucking oil out of the earth? Only for it to be turned into plastic to clog the earth in turn. Or burned to end up clogging the atmosphere. I dunno. Sometimes I feel it's destroying the world more effectively than anything else we've ever done.

— No wonder you quit your job!

— Yeah. It's always there. He pauses and sips his coffee, searching for the right word. Progress and regression. Creation, destruction.

She laughs and shakes her head, looks out the window and watches as a man in a pinstripe business suit presses a button and a handle shoots up from his wheelie bag.

— You know you're a total weirdo.

— I've always been one, he smiles and leans forward to kiss her playfully, and she accepts his kiss before shaking her head again to encourage him to sit back in his seat.

— I remember clearly the moment when my love of trains turned from being innocent to something more … realistic.

They are both smiling now and Sybille is happy right then because this is the way she has always liked it between them: he being slightly self deprecating but sharing himself at the same time, his guard down, and her getting insight into the way his mind works and how he experiences the world, so different from her own way of thinking yet warmly familiar.

— It was John –

— Ah! Of course it was John!

— He and I have always exchanged books. Guess it's a kind of showmanship.

— I'm sure it is.

— But seriously, he was the one to send me Zola's *La Bête Humaine*.

— Oh did he now? She is teasing again, smiling.

— Well, we always bonded over books and music. Ever since school.

— Bet you were the real cool kids, huh, she says sarcastically.

— Well, we were kind of, yeah. I didn't hang out with a lot of people. But John and me, we got along. Anyway, I was the first to get a job between the two of us. He posted me *La Bête Humaine* as a congratulations when I accepted the Aker Kvaener job in Oslo.

— Why that book?

— His note said: I always knew you loved trains, so this book is the book for you.

— And how did Monsieur Zola rob you of your innocence exactly?

William doesn't answer at first. Their train is finally departing and they lapse into silence as they watch the platform move and the train pass through the station.

— I'm not sure I had any innocence to be robbed, he finally says. That's the point. Complacency maybe.

— Complacency? Sybille asks, frowning. What do you mean?

— I think I had been complacent about what trains stood for. I mean, there are so many examples of engineering being put to use that's far from the engineer's mind. Zola was trying to make sense of this thing, this whole industry and the way of life it produced. The train was just fifty years old or so, less in the time his novel was set.

— Hard to imagine. Guess it's like us and the internet. I can't picture life without it and it's what, like, 30 years old?

241

— Yeah. I mean, think of it: by the twentieth century, trains were taken for granted. Armies all had mobilisation plans. Train timetables for war. Millions of soldiers.

They are now at Büchen, about to leave the länder of Schleswig-Holstein, around where the border would run between East and West Germany after 1949.

— You know, whatever about war, everything can be explained by trains, William says.

— Is that so? She leans her head back and asks sardonically: Is that why you always want to travel by train? You want to have the world explained to you?

— Trains gave us the First World War. They allowed America to connect its coasts. Stanford was a railroad man: his money gave us the university with his name, that gave us Silicon Valley, the internet. I mean, it's thanks to trains we discovered the second law of thermodynamics and that, basically, really does explain everything.

— And what – she is smiling and frowning at once – pray tell, is the second law of thermodynamics? Actually forget that, what the hell is the first law of thermodynamics?

— Heat cannot be created or destroyed because it's energy.

— Oh whatever! Strange man, you're boring me, she says but is smiling all the same.

There is a pause. They look at each other and he smiles and she looks away first, out the window, at the land rushing away, past and out of sight.

— The second law, he says somewhat triumphantly, states that heat will always move from an area where it is ordered to a place where it will be disordered. In an isolated system, entropy will always increase.

— And what the hell has that got to do with trains?

— Oh. He looks a little disappointed. Well it was thanks to trains that we discovered this.

William's head turns and he looks around him as if the current train they are on, the ICE T, is a cause of wonder and can itself answer Sybille's question of what the second law of thermodynamics has to do with trains.

— I mean, trains forced people like Carnot to work out how heat moves in one direction only.

— One direction only? Cold things get hot and then cold again all the time, that makes no sense.

— No but it takes work, energy, to warm things up.

— Like this coffee? Sybille asks after a moment's consideration, willing to indulge William's lecture. It's only going to ever get cold?

— Exactly. If you were to warm it up, you would need an external energy source.

— Like a microwave.

— And this accounts for time's arrow. Things move in one direction. Things fall apart: they don't fall together. Trains, they showed us this. Trains gave us this fact. They gave us standardised time.

Sybille purses her lips as if considering the possibility of the truth of all this, then asks, But what about life? I mean, we create so much, we're falling together all the time, and have babies. Children.

— Yes but we constantly are expelling energy as we do so. Look, think of the train and its steam engine. The piston and cylinder. A cyclical process. A decrease in entropy, it's order, but it's only achieved by the train expelling heat. If it didn't expel heat to the wider environment it would blow up or break down. We, too, are constantly expelling heat because we're working on breaking down the energy we consume in order to grow taller, or fatter, or have babies or whatever. Even thinking. We take in energy, break it down, use some of it for work, then expel it.

— What about the sun? It spontaneously makes things hot without any waste.

— Yes, well it's a free source of energy, it is true, but in that case it's still working. All of nature is striving toward equilibrium. All heat is cooling. The sun, too, will one day burn out.

— How cheerful.

— Well trains brought other things too.

— Not just war?

— And not just entropy. It's a dance, a two step. Two steps forward, one step back. Trains brought peace, prosperity, economic growth.

— I never really thought about trains like this, admits Sybille. I don't think I've been on a train outside of the city.

— You were never tempted to go interrailing?

— No, if I'm honest, not at all.

— David has spent a couple of summers interrailing. William smiles at the thought.

— And did you join him?

— No. The second time he went he wanted me to join him. But I bought a three-week ticket just for France. Which is not the same. And I travelled alone.

— Why only France?

— I guess I was attracted to the TGV. And besides, I couldn't stand his friends.

There isn't much time remaining of their journey. Their ICE T (t for tilting) class 411 train is speeding toward Spandau at a speed of two hundred and thirty kilometres an hour.

— Truth is, David was a bit out of control at that time and I found it hard to be in his company, William says solemnly. That year he had been constantly going out and falling behind on his lectures. I didn't want to think about him for the summer. So I went on my own.

He looks out the window and sees that the train is approaching Spandau on the edge of the city. Morning sun is shining bright across the buildings as they rush past out of sight. The other passengers start to stir and the elderly man Sybille helped in Hamburg now stands, stretching his legs and peering out at the same time. Tiergarten appears up ahead and Sybille turns in her seat to look out the opposite window, glimpsing the Victory Column, a reminder of the war the Prussians won against the French.

— I love you, you strange man, she says, turning back to face William and as she says these words she reaches for his hands and holds his in hers.

— I love you too, he says.

— Will you have my children?

To this sentimental banality William laughs and looks out the window and just then the conductor announces their arrival.

With thanks to: Adam Fearon, Alan Murrin, Jasmine Reimer, Mitch Speed and Anna Szaflarski for being this novel's first readers; thanks also to Adam for providing such excellent illustrative prints; Liza Costello for her excellent edit and feedback on the manuscript; Beata Niedhart and Oliver Spieker of Form und Konzept for the many years of collaboration and formidable design expertise; Mundi Vondi for the conversations and Juliet Barbieri, for the craic.

This book was written in various places between the years 2017–2023 and I would like to acknowledge the following for their hospitality: The Tyrone Guthrie Centre at Annaghmakerrig, Richard Mosse, Cill Rialaig Arts Centre, Nora Hickey M'Sichili and all the staff at the Centre Culturel Irelandais, Paris and most of all my mother Candy Holten, for everything, but also for having me during the time of pandemic.

Thanks also to the Arts Council of Ireland for their generous support.